The Burden

Also by Georg Engel from K A Nitz:

Thy Neighbour's Wife

The Famine Village and Other Tales

Sorceress Circe: A Berlin Romance

The Burden

Georg Engel

K A Nitz
WELLINGTON

Die Last first published
in German 1898

ISBN: 978-0-473-28235-6

Not to remain dependent on a person: and be they the most beloved — each person is a prison, also a corner.

— — Not to remain dependent on sympathy: and including higher men, in whose rare torment and helplessness, a destiny can be seen by us.

Friedrich Nietzsche, Beyond Good and Evil

Book One

The Burden

I

The day had begun. The rain was still drizzling and was dripping down onto the small windows of the invalid's room. Leaden grey light stole hesitantly through the curtains and mixed with the glow of the lamp which was also now burning before the bed.

Some life began to awake on the great farming estate. A dull hollering of the cows was occasionally heard, and, in between, the scattered calls of the servants. But everything sounded muffled, as if they were frightened of disturbing the invalid.

Something dead, depressed lay over the farmstead; and the more the dreary sunlight advanced, the greater the silence in which those present lapsed.

In the distant, ground floor room, a weak cry was heard. It sounded sickly, hollow, broken, a little irritated, but the voice also whispered so softly that immediately from the leather armchair next to the bed, a man of massive, imposing figure started, rubbed his eyes a little, brushed through his thick, short-cropped hair energetically a few times, and then laid his fingers cautiously on the hand of the suffering woman.

"Well, Else," he inquired encouragingly, whereby he muffled his voice as much as possible, "is it a little better?"

Instead of an answer, the woman wrung her hands, and buried her countenance in the pillows, "Dear God," she groaned softly, and it was almost as if a sob came out of the white linen.

The man let his hand sink onto his knee, and stared at the bright, sand bestrewn floor of the room.

Suddenly the young woman threw herself around, and inquired hastily, "You have surely slept, Wilms?"

Strange – the question seemed almost envious.

"Yes, I nodded off for a bit," her husband answered. And again, a gentle apology could be heard in the words. "I will soon also be sitting like this for the fourth night," he murmured half to himself.

It went quiet.

From the corner, only the heavy tick-tock of a hulking grandfather clock sounded, and the sand crunched occasionally under the man's boot.

The suffering woman sighed, and seemed unable to find the right position. Finally she stretched, and looked out into the comfortless grey of the rainy day.

What sadness out there and in here.

The rain whirled against the window, hailstones struck sharply against the panes, and a tear flowed over the cheeks of the woman lying there.

"Put the lamp out, Wilms," she asked, "my eyes – it hurts."

He turned the light down; it immediately looked even more ashen in the room.

"Poor woman," he murmured, "poor woman." He stroked her hair, and slowly stood up. Then he stepped to the door. – But he would not make it out.

"Wilms."

His wife had pulled herself together. "You shouldn't leave," she cried fearfully, "I cannot remain alone – I freeze when you are outside!"

"Else – our farm suffers as a result – I must –"

"Yes, yes — the farm — always the farm," the invalid burst out, and fell back exhausted onto her pillows, "and here I lie in my misery — two years — two whole years already, and no one helps me, no one, I fall as a burden on everyone — even you —"

"Else, I —"

"Yes, even you," she continued breathlessly, "I note it very well — you have only pity for me — only pity. And yet we married out of love."

He had stepped hesitantly to her bed, and suddenly she flung her arms around his neck, "Oh God — oh God, I am becoming very ugly surely?" she inquired, her entire body trembling. "Aren't I, just tell me straight."

"Else," — the man's voice trembled softly. He had sat down on the edge of the bed, and was letting a few strands of her long, blond hair glide through his fingers. "Else," he reassured her then, "for me you are still as beautiful as in the first hour — just look at your long, soft plaits — and your little mouth and dear, blue eyes — everything as pretty, my poor child."

It must have overwhelmed him though, for he enclosed his wife in both arms, and kissed her tenderly on the lips. The invalid huddled contentedly against his chest, and for a moment, she seemed enraptured and hopeful. At least, she soon turned to the side and asked him with her excited voice, "Wilms, give me the Bible from the table — so, and now go — just go and keep an eye on the farm — it must be."

Then the man walked ponderously out; only when he had shut the door, he paused and listened.

And he shook his head bleakly. — His wife was reading with such feverish, passionate fervour in there. She was almost singing; — ecstatic, as if intoxicated, she intoned the holy words, 'And, behold, a woman, which was diseased with an issue of blood twelve years, came behind him, and touched the hem of his garment. But

Jesus turned him about, and when he saw her, he said, Daughter, be of good comfort; thy faith hath made thee whole. And the woman was made whole from that hour.'*

"And was made whole from that hour," she repeated in there as if ecstatic. Then a moment of silence, but suddenly with heart-rending sobs, "Oh God — and was made whole — dear — dear — God."

II

When Wilms stepped out into the yard, he breathed deeply. Here fresh air was wafting, here the heat of the ill woman's room was no longer constricting him, and the rain drizzled refreshingly onto his exposed skin.

Strange. — He had stood so often in the middle of his yard, but today the thought befell him for the first time that all his possessions, houses and barns, stalls and equipment, men and cattle were as though entangled in an oppressive dream.

It crumbled and decayed everything, it turned rotten and died away. — And he himself?

Appalled, he started.

Over in the thatched roof of the corn barn, a considerable split was yawning. Unhindered, the rain was flowing through and rotting his winter seed. Nobody had reported the damage to him, he himself had not noticed it.

---

* Matthew 9:20–22.

The Burden

Previously he had been known as the most industrious farmer in Western Pomerania; he alone knew how to claim from the rich soil through magic three times as much of the golden, sustenance-bringing corn; now it was different. – It was going downhill with him.

A wagon lay in a corner of the yard on three wheels. The fourth broken next to it. – Had someone sent for the wheelwright?

Just then, a farm labourer crept idly behind the vehicle. Wilms called out loudly to him; but the man paid no attention, and already the farmer wanted to reprimand him with a vigorous oath, then he thought of the ill woman, and almost whispering, he ordered the man to fetch the wheelwright.

The labourer trotted away, and Wilms donned his rough cap and walked ponderously along the country road. His fields stretched out on both sides.

The rain rustled audibly on the brown loamy arable land, and only gradually was the farmer able to recognise his people, the heavy mist billowed so thickly around them. Grey and ghostly, men and women emerged from the clouds, and soon vanished again as if the ground were sucking them up.

"How are the potatoes, Karl?" Wilms finally asked a young, flax haired fellow who, stooped low, was throwing the collected tubers into a basket.

"Lord knows – the rain – it's already lasted too long."

"Yes, yes" – Wilms balled his fists, and deep creases furrowed into his serious, honest countenance. As he now sat down slowly and wearily on an iron plough which lay in the miry field, he could have been taken for an old, broken man. And he numbered just thirty two years, and stood in the prime of his powers.

And the mist crept around him, taking shape, balling, and it seemed as if an ugly, grey woman were forming, toothless, with waggling head — a gaunt hag, well known to all depressed people — hardship, grinning hardship, and she hobbled to him, and caressed him.

He sank down deeper and deeper into himself, and let his people do what they wanted.

Then the rattling of a wagon rang out along the country road. A wretched, groaning vehicle approached, and a corpulent man climbed down with grey stubbled beard, and in the stubble sat a very red, swollen face from which a pair of watery little eyes and a hook nose peered out jovially. The arrival was called Mr Rosenblüt, jingled at the moment a thick golden chain, and was the partner of one of the very well-known cattle export firms in the country town of Grimmen. — A tranquil, amiable man.

Today the cattle dealer appeared very upset however. He stepped straight up to the farmer, and planted himself snorting and huffing before him.

"Mr Wilms," he began abruptly, and waved his stick back and forth. "What does it mean? — What has happened — with you at home? When I was travelling past ..."

"But not my wife?" Wilms stammered, and sprang up — "isn't it? — Just tell me," the unfortunate man repeated hoarsely.

"No, no, not your wife — I just mean — — there is one of the men in blue, of the bailiffs. Come quickly to my wagon" — and he added softly, "Do you want to make a fracas before your people? Hurry up, Mr Wilms." Soon the vehicle was creaking and groaning to Wilms's farmstead, and Mr Rosenblüt sat next to the owner, and stared fearfully at his face until they had reached the farmyard.

Here the wagon stopped, and the farmer sprang down and looked around timidly.

In the middle of the place, the bailiff from Grimmen stood and negotiated loudly and brusquely with Jochen, the horse groom, who threw a fearful glance from time to time at the window of the ill woman's room, and seemed to beg the official to proceed more gently.

All the people of the estate were habituated in this respect to the suffering woman; a loud word in the midst of the silence was unheard of and seemingly startled everyone.

"There is our master," the groom said finally, relieved when he became aware of the farmer and his companion. Wilms approached ponderously, his figure collapsing more and more as if an all too heavy burden had been laid straight on his neck, and great drops were beading on his forehead. With whispering, hoarse voice, he asked the official to go with him into the next barn. — Just not here — here the ill woman could be disturbed, she must not know anything; that way she could get some rest. "I beg you, come with me — a few steps."

But the bailiff considered that to be excessive time-wasting. He unbuttoned his coat, took a stamped paper out, which he skimmed over, and while he stroked his military moustache officiously and with pleasure, he read drily aloud, "Charged by Count Brachwitz in Boltenhagen — payment of the rent in arrears from 1 April — 3,600 marks — — not received — hm — pre-emptive forced seizure."

"What? You are still owing the Count from April?" the cattle dealer threw out in between.

The bailiff folded the paper up again, and planted himself before the owner, "Can you pay, Mr Wilms?" he asked promptly.

"No."

"Well, then I must begin. Don't be offended."

"But — if you will just — let me have until tomorrow," Wilms groaned, and laid his hand over his forehead. "Just until tomorrow – I could still turn to somebody. – I have had so much with my wife in the last while – but it is perhaps still possible."

"I'm sorry – strict orders." The bailiff thereby buttoned up his coat, and turned to the groom.

"I'll start straightaway with the cattle," he ordered curtly. "Where do you have the pigs?"

"Then show the gentleman, Jochen." Wilms had spoken it mutely, and then turned away quickly. He had not even given the cattle dealer his hand in farewell. He walked slowly into the house, and stepped into his wife's room.

III

Else still lay just as he had left her. With her left hand, she was clasping the Bible, her right was fingering the wall nervously, and her morbidly illuminated eyes were directed at the window. The strange movement in the yard, the creaking of the doors, the grunting of the pigs now becoming louder, it all disturbed her. She was quite agitated, and when Wilms sat down next to her bed, she inquired breathlessly about the reason for all this noise. – – Yes, the reason. –

Was her husband permitted to betray the true cause to her? Was he able to confess that the best part of his possessions were now being taken away, that other debris would soon follow, and all the pillars of his house would collapse around him, around him, the strong, powerful man who had for years, as if lamed, been forged to this bed so firmly that all ability to move seemed hindered? – Strange, it seemed to him as if his wife were healthier than he was; and he was himself broken, haggard, powerless, a dead man who squatted in the large armchair and stared before himself.

"What are they doing so loudly outside?" his wife lamented, and slapped the covers nervously with the Bible – "shouldn't they have some consideration for me, Wilms?"

The farmer pulled himself together. Just spare the poor women, was his only thought. – The thought which called the hardship of his house to him.

"Eh, Else, it will soon stop again."

"Yes, but what are they doing?"

"Oh, Rosenblüt is just there and – and is buying cattle from me."

"The Jew?" the ill woman cried, and straightened up. – "Look – look there," she stuttered, and pointed straight out, "there he stands before the window – and looks in, straight at my bed." Horrified she fell back, and drew her covers up high so that she could not notice anymore how Rosenblüt beckoned with all sorts of grimaces to her husband. "Wilms, I cannot suffer that Jew – what do you always have with him. Constantly something. The Pastor says too that you give too much to him."

"Quiet, Else, I have already earned a lot of money from the man."

"Certainly not – they betray everyone. You just don't understand the business." – Those were wicked words.

Wilms started, and grasped his chest. Outside Mr Rosenblüt was waving more and more energetically.

"I must go into the yard for a moment now, Else," the man encouraged himself finally.

"Again already?"

She threw a fleeting look at him and grasped his hand, "You have only just come in. – And then – I am always so well when you are by me, but as soon as you leave me alone, then the terrible fear overcomes me – you know – as if something were sitting on my chest" – she wheezed – "you will stay, won't you?"

He remained, and collapsed without answer into the tall armchair. It was the picture of his life. – The burden pulled at him and drew him down.

Now she spoke, and kept asking ever hastily. How was it with the farm? – Good though? And the Pastor had brought her an advertisement in which a wheelchair was touted at a not too expensive price. 150 marks. "That isn't too much, is it? – You could spare that for your wife? You are fond of me? Aren't you?" – And then came the memories. How she had frisked about still fresh and healthy in her household, and how terribly in love Wilms had acted as a young husband. Behind every door, where the staff could not see, he had begged for a kiss. "Oh, kiss me again like that. – I am actually still as young."

Half numb, his head sank onto her breast. He was so shattered that he did not possess a full appreciation for anything anymore.

Then there was a knocking at the door. First gently, then energetically, and finally Mr Rosenblüt stepped into the room, and looked around the ill woman's room disconcertedly. The dull air and the picture of the husband and wife holding each other in their embrace left him silent for a moment, a sort of stirring ignited in the dealer's features, but then the time urged too powerfully and he cleared his throat loudly, "Good morning – Mrs Wilms – I beg your forgiveness – how goes it with you? – but it's high time, Mr Wilms – I must speak with you, now immediately. The fellow is ruining your entire business."

The strange voice hit Else like a shot.

"Good God, who is it?" the ill woman stammered when she perceived the intruder who made a stiff bow towards her, and over her face flooded a burning redness, "What does he want here? – Wilms, my room is not for business? Why don't you go with the gentleman into the living room?"

It was an unfriendly greeting, and Mr Rosenblüt stood as though thunderstruck. Only when Wilms seized him by the arm, and asked kindly that he follow him did the dealer pull himself together so far as to be able to wave his hat energetically and flare up excitedly, "What? Then I can go too. Adieu, Mr Wilms, give my regards to your revered wife." But Wilms did not let him go, and with much begging and apologising, he shoved him out of the room through a brown lacquered door in whose middle was placed a large, oval windowpane covered by a curtain. In the living room stood simple green rep covered furniture, embroidered covers were resplendent on the sofa, and a large beam covered in wallpaper ran across the middle of the ceiling. Here Wilms fell down into one of the upholstered chairs, propped his head in his hand, and finally asked his business friend what he wished, but it sounded as absent-minded, as distant and muted, as if the man's spirit were wandering on dreary paths of madness. And this brokenness, this complete dozing of a previously great power shook the other man. Half pitying, and half timorous, he stepped towards him. Then he touched the shoulder of the seated man with his stick, and while he now incessantly struck him softly on the shoulder, he talked insistently to him. It was a long lecture, but Wilms only heard one thing, and that was something hopeful in the midst of his comfortless night, an early red shimmer, a flashing light. – Mr Rosenblüt was outraged over the seizure. – The official would certainly have taken double the value from the business, the best looking cattle without which the owner could not continue to exist at all. His indignation was so honest, it just streamed out of him. – "What is it all about? – The Count is making a fortune from it? – The best animals – sleight of hand. – Wilms, do you know something? I will pay you the 3600 marks, and you will put aside the pawned animals for me. And if you cannot refund the money to me in eight days, then, now then it will all belong to me. – That is a speculation. – I am a businessman – that is a business – will you?"

"Yes, yes." Oh, it was to the sweltering man as if a friendly hand had offered him a drink of cold water after a dusty wandering. He felt seemingly as if something refreshing was trickling unhurriedly through him. He slowly stood up, and stretched. – Eight days time – a whole week yet? – Yes, rescue must come by then, from somewhere, all the same, in any case for the time being, the most appalling burden had rolled from his soul. Breathing deeply, his chest rose and fell quickly.

"Yes, old friend, of course, I accept it, with a thousand delights, deliver it."

But the dealer paused for a moment suspiciously.

"Mr Wilms, don't take offense, I still have a condition."

"Oh, surely because of the interest?"

"Forbid – it will be find, understand, interest too. No, it concerns something else, but that I will tell you later. Now go outside, and make an arrangement for your things with the bloodsucker outside. – Onwards."

With that he counted out a number of banknotes onto the table. Wilms snatched at them, and strode out without another word into the yard where the bailiff had just concluded his work in the barn.

In a few minutes, the surprised man held the contentious sum in his hand, wrote a receipt whilst still standing, shook Wilms' hand, sprang onto his wagon, and rattled off from the yard.

The work of a moment, it was all like a transitory, nasty dream. Wilms and Rosenblüt stood under the rotten gate and watched after the disappearing vehicle. But when it had disappeared behind the fir copse into a depression in the country road, the dealer planted himself in front of his serious business friend, stuck his hand in his pocket, and rattled with his stick back and forth in the palings of the fence.

"Listen to me, old friend," he finally began restively, and spat in front of himself. "Now I also want to tell you what I desire from you. If I should be unconcerned about my money, then you must pay attention exclusively to your business again. – And you can only do that if you get yourself a stand-in with your wife. A carer, or something similar. There are nurses enough. I can also look around in Grimmen for one."

Wilms brushed his forehead with his hand. What he had just heard rang out like a brazen indictment in him. "Yes, yes," he murmured half to himself, "I have already thought of that – but it won't work."

"Won't work?" Mr Rosenblüt began to get angry. "Well, why not then?"

"Because my wife won't tolerate a stranger in the house. – I must do her will, the poor, tormented woman."

"Dammit, then get a relative to come. – And yes – listen to me" –

The speaker suddenly straightened up, and struck the farmer energetically on the shoulder – "Thunderbolts, something occurred to me then. Wilms, your little sister-in-law just returned a few days ago from Stralsund. I just saw her climbing out of the wagon as she went into your father-in-law's house. A strapping thing, so tall" – Mt Rosenblüt indicated an enormous height – "take her – she will create order here. Well, and if you want, I will myself speak a few words with the old man in Grimmen. – Well then?"

Wilms was gripped. He stared steadily at the dealer with his bushy browed, blue eyes and pondered. He indeed hardly knew his wife's younger sister. When he had been courting Else, little Hedwig had been a sixteen year old, taciturn, shy girl to whom he had not paid much heed. Yes, he thought to himself, her peculiarly lurking, secretive being had sometimes irritated him, but yet – the practical dealer had obviously hit on the right idea.

Else could not object to her sister. And above all things: he would become free, free and unhindered for his arduous trade. – He wavered for a moment more, once more he quickly scanned the window to the invalid's room, then he declared decisively to the dealer that he would follow his advice. That very day, a letter would go out to the farmer's father-in-law, the old rentier Schröder in Grimmen.

"Bravo! – a man is as good as his word, Mr Wilms," the businessman reminded imperatively as he climbed onto his waiting wagon, "isn't he?"

The man addressed nodded with his massive head, "Don't worry, Mr Rosenblüt."

"And when I return, it will look differently here," the parting man called back, then a handshake, and the second wagon also rolled away.

Wilms, however, stood in the middle of the country road, and gazed after it.

A strange, apprehensive joyfulness befell him. And slowly and thoughtfully, he stepped back into the house.

IV

It was a Sunday. The rain had stopped. A fresh wind was passing over the autumn fields. The blue sky stretched out wide and vast, and over the trees and bushes, paths and trails lay bright sunshine.

From the station clock of the tiny secondary train station of Boltenhagen, it struck eleven. – Around this hour, Wilms's young sister-in-law had to arrive.

Behind the wooden shed which acted as the waiting room, although it was completely uncovered and lay out in the middle of the open fields, the leaseholder had already been waiting for quarter of an hour with a comfortable wicker carriage, and was gazing reflectively at the shiny rails which glistened and sparkled in the sunlight.

He thought about whether something good would surely roll towards him on the iron path. Whether he would find in Hedwig that support and help which he sought. – Strangely, as often as he thought of the girl, the same unpleasant feeling which had infused him when she was a child befell him again. – – But she could have changed in the meantime. Two years brings a lot, and she had surely polished herself exceedingly in the Stralsund boarding house. Naturally, it was ridiculous to brood constantly over this instinctive dislike.

No, he wanted – – –

An elegant hunting carriage drove up at this moment, and startled the farmer out of his deliberations. With dignity, the coachman climbed from the carriage in a rich, ornate silver livery, and Wilms realised that the lord of the manor, Count Brachwitz, the very one who insisted so strictly on collecting the lease money, must likewise be expecting a guest. But the farmer was not curious, the coachman strode loftily past him, and at the same time, a rapid puffing and blowing announced the approach of the train. With a spring, Wilms was by the rails, the station bells rang, and a pair of wagons stopped slowly and screeching in the middle of the open fields. And then – from a carriage, a slender and at the same time full and strongly grown girl's figure sprang out quickly and lithely, looked around, and recognised with a single, clear, purposeful glance the waiting man.

"Brother-in-law."

Wilms listened attentively. The voice sounded so fresh and bright, so full of volition, almost as if she were accustomed to giving commands. – Strange, the girl had also travelled second class; that was a lady. And when he now finally stood before her, stretched out his hand to her, and emitted a few awkward words of greeting, a pair of large, brown eyes shone up into his for a moment, then she ingenuously reached for his mouth, and with a certain painful anxiety, the big awkward man had to bend down to kiss the lips of a person almost a stranger to him. A shivery, unpleasant feeling stole up on him at the same time. – And this excellent figure would run the farm with him? – Quickly he took her small handbag, and was wanting to lead her just then to his wagon when he was addressed by a young gentleman in hunting clothes who placed himself laughing in his path.

"Stop, Mr Wilms, not so quick – well, man, don't you recognise your old friend anymore?" At the same time, the hunter doffed his green cap politely before Hedwig while he tossed his double-barrelled shotgun adroitly on a strap over his shoulder. As he stood there thus, he formed the type of a handsome, young, elegant aristocrat, with his black moustache on the brown face, and with the casual awareness of his strength peculiar to his caste. Behind him, a liveried servant waited with hat removed, and a brown hunting dog was snuffling around the young lord's pockets.

"Fritz – Count" – Wilms burst out.

"Well," the huntsman cut him off, and shook the leaseholder's hand cheerfully, "Tell me, how you're feeling. Out here it's not working out. – Have had to acknowledge it in fact – papa's wish, do you understand? So that I would become prudent on the estate. As if I weren't already so prudent that it could make a dog wail," he added, and turned again to Wilms's companion.

"The young lady probably doesn't think of me anymore?" he continued ingratiatingly. "Not even of the boarding house ball where I had the fortune of being the favoured dancer several times – really not? – Admittedly, when you're so besieged." And again he doffed his cap affectionately. – "Are you familiar then with Mr Wilms, related, by marriage, or what?"

"Yes, I am the gentleman's sister-in-law," the girl informed him politely, and yet the farmer heard again a cool unapproachable tone which was more fitted to a countess than the daughter of the rentier Schröder from Grimmen. Even the young Count stared for a moment sheepishly at her face, then he seemed suddenly not to find any more enjoyment in the conversation, for he looked around for his servant without paying any more consideration to the girl and, as he stuck a cigar in his mouth, asked with an indistinct murmur for a light.

"Good – burning already – well, till we meet again, Wilms" (he casually forgot the 'Mister') "– had the honour, my lady – here, Hector." He whistled to the dog, farewelled them airily, and sprang onto the carriage whose reins he grasped. Behind him sat the coachman, and with elegant, inaudible rolling, the vehicle flew away.

Then, where the country road turned off into the fir copse, the hunter looked around again, and peered back sharply. Hedwig, who had already taken her place on the wicker carriage next to Wilms, noticed it, a bold, mocking smile flew around her fresh lips, ever secretly observed by the farmer who sat turned into himself next to her and drove. Timidly, he sometimes looked at her from the side. How did the young girl come by such friendships? — She seemed to know the young lord better than she wanted to admit? And why did she act towards him with such superiority? Wilms sighed deeply. No, it was not the person whom he needed to nurse Else and help him in the business. His first instinctive reluctance had been warranted. As she now sat next to him, her slender figure bent a little forward, her large, brown eyes directed thirstily into the sunlit distance, her lips open as if she were drinking the inrushing air, she seemed to him to be too fine, too foreign a being.

"My God, what will Else say about it?" he thought, distressed. "And about the sort of hat she wears, and the gloves?"

He whipped heftily at the horse like someone who wanted to bring something unpleasant quickly to an end, and the vehicle rolled on at a sharp trot without Hedwig having interrupted the embarrassed silence.

Just once she asked almost indifferently, her eyes always directed into the distance, "Is Else still as pretty as she was?"

Wilms bit his lip, the reins in his hand loosened involuntarily.

Had he heard correctly? Her fresh, clear voice chimed exactly as cool, as uppish, as completely disinterested as if her question was being applied to a quite insignificant person.

And it was her sister who had inquired after his poor tormented wife?

"Yes," he burst out roughly, "just as pretty – just as – – admittedly, she can't go for walks, or clean anymore."

Those few words sounded accusatory and scathing, and Hedwig directed her eyes for the first time at her brother-in-law. She seemed astonished, and curled her lips up a little. And almost with deliberate sourness, she added, "Her long illness has surely cost a lot of money?"

Wilms swallowed his displeasure. Like a raging man, he whipped at the animal, driving it into an extended gallop.

The two did not speak anymore with each other. They passed through the village in uncomfortable silence, until they finally arrived at the leased farm.

It lay there dreamy, dilapidated, and soundless as ever. And this deathly silence enticed the first word from Hedwig.

"Strange," she murmured timidly, as Wilms offered her his hand to climb down, "I had thought it'd be different. Is it always so silent here?"

"Yes, my child, always. Out of consideration for Else. And then it is also Sunday today."

"Yes, so – so, so," she repeated to herself, bothered. Wilms saw that she was scanning the premises again with one of her long, clear looks. Then she brushed her forehead, and uttered quickly and urgently, as if she wanted to escape the view, "Come – we will go to my sister."

V

The afternoon was in a dozy state. In the yard, grey shadows were already weaving and creeping up the walls of the barn, but in the ill woman's room, a large, beautiful floor lamp burned, a wedding present which had never been used, and it now spread a radiant, cosy light.

"Here it has to be doubly bright," the younger sister had opined, and then the floor lamp had simply been taken down from the glass cabinet, and repaired.

Quiet and contented, the ill woman now lay in her bed, and looked with blinking eyes into the beams of light while her slender fingers held firmly onto the hand of her sister sitting next to the bed.

In the middle of the room, before the large table, Wilms had taken his place, and bent eagerly over an account book which had been neglected for many months. The big man was only slowly and ponderously capable of calculating, but it did him untold benefit to finally be able to bring clarity to his circumstances again. Thus he toiled onward, and only from time to time did he raise his head and listen to the two women.

Over there Hedwig was reading aloud to the ill woman. Oddly, not from the Bible. The new nurse had immediately declared that it was not expedient to recite to a sufferer something which she knew almost by heart, and which pointed her thoughts constantly to death and transience. – No, something new and cheerful must be chosen, and she had immediately scurried into her room in the loft to bring what she had promised. – When she returned after some time, she had also changed her dress. – A black garment lay simply and loosely around her slender body, and made her appear still stronger and more self-aware than before. Smiling she sat down by the bed, and began to read aloud. It was the story, written by a modern, Swedish satirist, of a young girl dallying with two lovers at the same time, only to finally marry for money, into which she brought as her only dowry both the abandoned lovers with her as man-friends.

Else did not really understand the allusions. – She had sat up in her pillows, and followed the subtle railleries with contented astonishment. Occasionally even a weak smile flittered over her pale face.

How long Wilms had yearned for such a benign sign, and now the poor thing seemed almost to have forgotten her suffering.

The farmer was also spontaneously caught in the gentle words which streamed so fresh and bright from Hedwig's lips. He supported his head, and looked over at her attentively. – And yet – while he listened to her lively recital with pleasure, that inexplicable aversion to the girl was gnawing gently again at his straightforward nature, an aversion he could not dispel, and which seemingly stalked him.

Already as she sat there, leaning back deeply in her chair so that every form of her fresh young body led a battle against the restricting garment, so loose, so without consideration for him, as if he were not present at all, her head tilted to the side, and in her features all that shifting, prickling mockery as if the contents of the book were reflected in her fine face, – it all did not belong here, not in the Pomeranian room of an ill woman, it was something impure, intolerable. – And now he felt also how cheeky and unfitting what she read was.

The redness climbed up to his brow. He rose ponderously, walked up and down the room several times, and finally cleared his throat heavily, "Should we stop the reading now?" And then the unexpected happened.

"No," – Else shivered, and shook her head unwillingly, "You are always having to disturb things," she complained. – "Let us have our enjoyment. I am so happy that I am getting a little variety." – And again she squeezed her sister's hand.

That as well.

The leaseholder murmured something incomprehensible to himself, he wanted strongly to reply, but the habit of sparing his wife by all means was stronger. He arduously mastered his rising fury, and left the room with heavy steps.

When he shut the door, he heard the girl reading on again loudly and with delight.

He ran about outside in the darkness for a few hours, always along the country road, and sought to shake off his temper.

Straight on the first day, she had brought unease and disquiet into the house. He had known in advance. – The girl just did not fit into the limited circle. Whether it would not be for the best to induce her to go again? – He sighed – – that must unfortunately not be attempted. – And then, how indifferently and scornfully she treated him himself. The shoulder shrug and the speaking away from him. He was just a 'farmer' to the girl.

"Ha – ha!" The leaseholder paused abruptly, and breathed deeply. – Quite different worries than this strange girl beset him. How could he have forgotten it for a moment?

The debt burden – the horrific debt. Eight days respite he had, in this time he had to make 1,200 talers, otherwise the entire inventory belonged to the Jew. But from where? – from where?

He groaned loudly, and the despair grasped him so heftily again that he embraced a poplar by the country road, and shook and kicked the strong trunk until a cloud of withered leaves rustled down on him.

A cold night wind swept through the branches, everything was dark and quiet. Only the leaves up above began rustling together again.

Was it not as if a man were speaking?

Hedwig's voice — he perceived it distinctly again up above, reading, laughing, and giggling.

The solitary man shivered, and listened. — Yes, there was something sick in him, it hurt in his chest. And lightning quick, the consciousness passed through him that the ill woman at home whom he loved so passionately, so deeply, so careworn, had turned him into a weakling, that this pale, haggard woman had stolen his strength, that she sucked his blood daily to thereby prolong her existence, just like that ghostly bird of which he had learnt as a boy, that bites the veins of the dying.

"God save me — Else — Else, what is it with me?" Wilms stammered, and wiped the sweat of fear from his brow — "home — home."

He ran, he stormed along until, with gasping breath, he had reached the deserted, slumbering yard. On his toes, he then crept through the hall, and soundlessly opened the door to the room.

A night light was burning on the table. From the half darkness, from which the restive breaths of the invalid trembled, a slender figure rose, and silently approached the intruder.

Now Hedwig stood before him. She laid her finger on her lips, and murmured curtly, "She is sleeping — I will keep watch over her today."

"You?"

"Yes."

"You? No, I — I don't want that."

The girl suddenly bent forward so that he felt her breath.

"And why not?"

Despite the darkness, their looks met, and remained hanging on each other astonished and questioning. Then the hour rolled; the recumbent woman stirred, and then — Wilms stepped back, and murmured wearily, “For my sake.”

With that he closed the door to feel his way quietly outside up the creaking stairs to the room under the thatched roof where he had often spent the night before.

And he felt so languorous and exhausted that he did not present himself with the question of why he gave in to the girl.

Up in the bare, whitewashed room, he undressed quickly, and soon lay stretched out in the high bed, but without being able to find the rest he desired.

The low ceiling almost pressed against his head, and again and again he lifted his head and listened to the moaning and whistling of the wind sweeping over the roof wailing.

It sounded just like the groaning of a tortured, gigantic body.

VI

The tenth hour of the morning had already broken when Hedwig stepped into the room which she had left shortly before, a modern little hat over her brown hair, and above her waist an elegant, open jacket which emphasised her fullness quite well.

She pulled on her gloves, and at the same time she peered attentively out the window as though looking at the weather.

"You want to go out?" the invalid inquired with gentle reproach while a cloud flew across her brow, for the pitiable woman had already won the firm conviction that she felt better in the presence of her sister.

"Yes," the younger woman replied breathing out, and without especially heeding the hidden rebuke, "it is so fresh outside today – really splendid – threads of summer drawing everywhere – just look – and here inside –" she did not finish, but quickly added, "I am not yet so well used to keeping watch – and you are better today – so I want to take a walk across your farm today. I will be back again in an hour."

"But Hedwig, when I'm so alone –"

"I'll bring you back something nice too," the other woman cut her off smiling, and had vanished the next moment.

Sighing, the abandoned woman sat up, and looked yearningly through the windowpanes at the slender girl's figure which was already striding without particular haste with easy vigorous movements across the yard.

"Anyone who also so –," the ill woman finally whispered, "just once, just once – –" She folded her hands convulsively, and her soul rose again into that one ardent prayer to God.

Meanwhile Hedwig had measured out the yard. Anyone who saw her thus, with the elegant, thin parasol in her hand, and her modern clothes, would hardly have believed that not the smallest blemish in the thatched roof of a barn escaped the brown, sparkling eyes of this young lady.

She noticed everything. She even seemed to sense an interest for the tiniest thing in this silent farm.

Before the open cow stalls from which a warm haze exuded, an old, weatherbeaten man crouched on a kerbstone, an ancient, scrawny, toothless human who sat there waggling his head, and seemed to be sunning himself. Next to him on his wooden clogs, a dishevelled raven stood on one leg, and was likewise sunken in the general leaden sleep which surrounded the entire small property as though accursed.

"Old man," Hedwig called when she had reached him, and tapped gently with her parasol on the ground, "Why does the yard look so messy?"

"Hey?" the old man grunted, and lifted his ear in the manner of the hard of hearing. At the same time, his extinguished, stupid eyes blinked up at the fresh, blossoming girl's face, and his toothless mouth began chewing.

The young, strong life there before him obviously did not please him. She also spoke to him with too little respect, for old Krischan had been consuming the charity of the farm since before living memory, and had in addition a reputation for dark, secret arts. The raven was deemed to be a sort of evil spirit serving him, or at least a confederate in all sorts of black deeds.

"Quick – take a broom, and sweep up everything properly," the beautiful girl suddenly called out urgently in the meantime. It seemed to her as if everything ugly and sick that she discovered here could be turned around with a strong hand.

The old man did not stir.

She prodded him.

Then a soft grimace drew over the wrinkled face, the mouth lifted into a grin, and without stirring from his place, he hoarsely wheezed his answer, "Work? – no, past – all long past – no, no, my daughter, if you want to turn something around here, then you must do it yourself."

"And you, what do you do here?" Hedwig called sharply in reply. Her entire body was shaking. The slack idleness of the old man outraged her.

"Me? – I'm waiting for death."

"For death?"

The aggressor blanched instinctively, and stepped back. The old man threw a squinting angry look at her, and the raven rose suddenly, and struck croaking and hacking with its wings at her.

It was as if the old times wanted to defend themselves in this yard against her.

Only the new arrival was not the sort to let herself be influenced for long by those sorts of obscure ideas.

She lifted her head proudly, and let the words fall coolly, "I will speak with my brother-in-law about you."

In the next moment, she turned, and hurried out to the country road without farewell.

How fresh and bright it was here outside. Above her the unending, bright blue, before her the fields and pasture, green and brown expanses, the one still in ripe adornment of late sowing, the other already ploughed again, between them little, bright rivulets like silver ribbons on a colourful cloth, scent and half-light, and blue misted forests in the distance, and above everything the morning wind whispering over the ground, carrying a powerfully earthy smell with it.

Hedwig sucked it in deeply. The little incident with the old man was already forgotten. She set off briskly over the ditches of the country road, and turned into the first best field path which ran diagonally across a field of stubble on which a few dark points were wavering back and forth in the uncertain distance.

How lonely it was everywhere here. Only a flock of crows were hopping about on the reaped ground, and at a turning she saw sitting on a wild thorn bush a delicate, colourful goldfinch singing its vigorous melody in the sunshine. Otherwise a blessed agreeable calm wove over everything.

Hedwig stopped, and let her eyes scan all around.

Thus she would spend her days here from now on? So alone, so exposed among strange people? For her dry mind told her that even Else would remain a stranger to her, a pitiable woman for whom she could at most be able to force an unpleasant feeling of pity.

And the soundless loneliness began to depress her.

Like something shadowy, it flew across the heath, came up to her, and tormented and scared her.

She thought of her last stay in the Stralsund boarding house and, shivering, she again felt that one incident before which her previous life had collapsed, that one appalling hour to which all her thoughts had firmly attached, so firmly that her body actually wandered about half in dream, almost separated from a guiding soul. And she felt again that she had to forget something in her life, and that this broad wasteland all around could perhaps produce that dull submissiveness in her which she yearned for.

And strange. — As she pondered this dark distant dream, she aroused something there. — A fleeing hare crossed her path, turned back before her, and then set off to the side over the field.

The girl suddenly laughed brightly.

The fresh, self-assured laughter of a vigorous person. Why did she need to be caught up in such mental webs? It was all over, would soon be no more, just a strange flickering memory. She hurried on with raised head; she struck back and forth with her parasol playfully at the bushes bordering the path, and then she paused again to let her cheeks be cooled by the swishing wind.

Thus she arrived in a narrow defile. The field rose almost to a man's height above her on both sides. On the sides, wild roses still blossomed, entire reddish brown bundles of heather sprouted there, and here and there violet bellflowers nodded in between.

Without thinking, the girl plucked a bouquet, perhaps intended for her own breast, perhaps for Else, then she heard unexpectedly up above voices becoming loud, and an altercation developing.

And now she also recognised who was speaking there. It was Wilms, who seemed to be being reminded by his day labourers of an outstanding debt.

Four to five men were talking over each other up above.

"People, I have given you what I had – now be patient a few days – you know all that I had to meanwhile undergo – a little while, then everything will be balanced up again. – Right?"

"Yes, sir, we have trust in you too, but it looks lean at home for us too."

"Eh we don't want to hustle you – that we won't do –"

"No, Mr Wilms, you have always been good to us, and we would surely not have now alone, – just wife and children –"

"They can't go hungry, sir."

There was silence for a moment. The men seemed to have paused, and the listener heard again how the wind skimmed through the heath's vegetation. Then the leaseholder said with his deep ingenuous voice, "Come to me tomorrow evening, people, then you will definitely receive your money – at all events." And in a firmer tone, he added, "And now go back to your work."

"Well, then we thank you many times, sir. Adieu!"

"Have a good morning."

She heard how the day labourers went away, and somewhat later Hedwig noticed that heavy steps were crunching down the defile.

Now he must be there. Instinctively the girl stepped back behind the thorn bush as if she wanted to let the approaching man pass undisturbed.

The leaseholder too had no idea of the nearness of another being who could investigate him and his torment, otherwise he would certainly have stridden past quickly; but he thus pulled up at the deepest part of the path, sank his head onto his chest and, with a weary, slack motion, pressed his hand against his forehead.

So much weariness lay in it, so much locked up woe.

But no groan streamed over his closed lips, the large figure remained soundless, without words, it was a lament made between him and God alone, hidden and protected by the solitude.

No strange eye was permitted to catch sight of its like.

With her cool, sharp look, Wilms's sister-in-law had grasped all of this, now she saw how the leaseholder drew the grey forester's jacket tighter, set his superintendent's cap right and continued with a firm step.

Thank God. It was also better thus.

Soon he must disappear.

And yet – her destiny urged her suddenly, almost against her will, to intervene in the fate of this man.

He had already reached the higher lying area.

A stone loosened from the embankment where the girl stood, and rolled with a clatter down into the defile.

Wilms turned back with a jerk.

Was he deceiving himself? The young, elegantly dressed woman down there was really – yes, it was Hedwig, she must have overtaken him earlier.

The leaseholder's features twisted, something brutal climbed up in them, and the veins in his eyes became bloody.

"How did you get there?"

"Me?" — she dangled the parasol carelessly, and came nearer — "I was going for a little walk."

"Why don't you stay with Else?"

"Because I could not bear it any longer — the watching over, I think, was straining me too much."

Wilms erupted, "And now you walk here so — so — what are you actually doing here?"

He had leant forward, his lips shaking.

But something suddenly awoke in the girl, something before which she was herself terrified, and of which she had thought so strongly before.

She stepped up quite close to the upset man, and threw him a solitary look, "I told you, I am going for a walk," it came forth sharp and defiant.

Her fists were balled in the delicate glacé leather, her body shook.

In that moment she resembled a cat gathering for a spring. From her flickering eyes glowed the desire to wrestle with her oppressor. Chest to chest. For something unrecognised — precious — for herself.

All that was to the rough, kindhearted farmer so new, so inconceivable, that he stared at the head trembling with fury before him for some minutes shaking his head.

"What do you actually want from me?" he murmured finally uncomprehending.

"Me?"

She awoke suddenly as if from an agreeable dream, and a burning redness ran across her features.

Both stared at each other still as though fallen from the heavens. Slowly the girl let her raised parasol glide down, and straightened up firmly.

A scornful trait flew around her fresh lips.

It was surely her destiny to have to contend everywhere with men in real, physical struggle. This one here did not at least seem dangerous.

"I wanted to speak with you about your circumstances," she began curtly and drily.

He stood so tall and powerful, and yet so awkwardly before her.

Oh, how it excited her to let this unruly giant feel her might.

"Over my circumstances?" the leaseholder repeated, cold sweat rising on his forehead.

"Then you heard all of it before, really all of it?"

"Yes, I know that you find yourself pressed for money."

The painful silence lasted for a second longer, the man's chest rose and fell as if he wanted to roll something away from himself, his head protruded like a steer, his teeth ground together mechanically.

Then it burst out of him.

"And you — why are you interfering here, you cheeky girl? — — — What concern is all that of yours? No, no, you must go, — from the house — today."

Did he really scream and roar all this invective in the girl's face? No, oh no, the words thrust through his brain faint and painful, but over his half open lips poured dull and hoarse only the following, "What concern is that of yours? — What of it all? Why are you thrusting yourself into my affairs? Well?"

"Why? — Because I want to get clarity over the people with whom I shall be living from now on."

"Want — you really want to stay with us? — Hedwig — but — but you — you don't fit in at all here, you are no good in such sadness — you should rather go again."

Both had spontaneously taken the path anew, and were striding next to each other over the empty heath.

The man sunken in himself, the girl slenderly upright and lithe, fastening an inquiring look from time to time on her companion.

And again he said insistently to himself, “Yes, yes, you should go.”

Then Hedwig seized his arm, and laid her own in it.

It was the movement and manner like she had learnt it up in the aristocratic dance hours in the old Hanseatic town.

Furrowing his brow, Wilms let it happen, but inwardly this elegant bearing infuriated him, although it had light and graceful enough an effect.

“Brother-in-law, do you really have something against me?” she suddenly asked, and let her clever brown eyes rest firmly on him.

Her arm was still pressing against his so that she had to notice his fright. The lies which would now be needed brought the honest man into total confusion.

“I — no, — what are you thinking, — I have nothing against you.”

“And Else?”

“My poor wife surely nothing either — just —”

He faltered, and that great embarrassment spread over his open features again.

“Just — now then?”

“Now, you are surely only too superior to us” — he stammered. “You have enjoyed so much education — over in the fine boarding house — Else and I, we are only simple people. And then my narrow income, you have heard it yourself, it will not cover you in the long run.”

She huddled close to him until he could almost feel her soft limbs, and whispered quickly and with an expression of concern, “But I would like so much to apply my powers for you, I am strong, brother-in-law, and would like to help you.”

“Really?” he started, and turned fully to her. “You want to do that indeed?”

She nodded, and looked at him seriously. “And spread a bit of ease and comfort with you again. You are missing that?”

The leaseholder made no reply, but he sighed deeply and gazed inwardly, turned towards the edge of the forest which they were now nearing.

But Hedwig hung tighter to him, and continued with interest, “You were yourself earlier certainly much more cheerful?”

“Yes, earlier” — the farmer repeated, fetching a deep breath — “earlier — it may well have been so. At the time, we were still good things. Then I often also walked with Else across the fields — —”

“Like now?” she threw quickly in between.

Wilms let a timid glance glide over her, and released his arm awkwardly from hers. “Yes, my child, almost so,” he said bleakly. And after a pause, he added almost disparagingly, “You actually don’t look like her at all.”

“No,” his companion confirmed.

It sounded sharp and sour.

Wordlessly the pair entered the forest path next to each other.

It was a widely dispersed pine forest with regularly hewed out paths which cut through the forest like narrow roads and seemed to peter out in the half-light.

The tips of the trees were immersed in bright sunlight, and waved back and forth in the gentle breeze. A strong smell of sap arose from the trunks. From a distance, the monotonous sound of falling axes could be heard. And a jay was crying loud and strong in the air.

The two people, so strange to one another, had already penetrated far into the solitary, slumbering forest when Hedwig unprompted began the conversation anew. Her figure straightened up at the same time, her dark eyebrows knitted together, her entire being seemed to be dominated by a firm resolve.

"Where are you going now?" she enquired curtly.

And just this tone, the farmer could not bear. Ill-temperedly he shook his head, and seemed to have heard nothing.

She suddenly stopped.

He turned back unwillingly and beckoned, but she did not stir from the place.

In her narrow fitting jacket, her modish hat and her blossoming face under it, she appeared strange from between the tall, ancient pine trees.

"Where are you going, I would like to know?"

And strangely, her glance met his own so firmly and seriously, they stood so close opposite each other again, that it became painful for the man.

"To the forester," he replied, and he spontaneously murmured after that, "I want to sell him hay."

"You need the money surely for the day labourers from before. Right?"

How she guessed it. How practically the girl thought, it did the suffering man quite well that she came to the right conclusion.

"Yes, yes," he burst out full of fear, "if he would only like to buy it."

A high spirited trait glided around the fresh, somewhat curled lips of the girl. "He will," she replied definitely, "does he have a wife?"

"Yes, married young."

"Good, then I will go with you, and seek to deputise the wife."

"Oh yes, Hedwig, that would be – very nice – of you –" he stuttered with downfallen eyes.

A hot feeling was climbing in him, something like gratitude, something like the delight of being attached to a being that wanted to help him. And yet – large drops of shameful sweat were beading at the same time on his forehead. She noticed it, and asked him to show her the way. Without objection, he let it happen that she placed her arm under his own, and he hurried with her then tempestuously forward in unusual haste.

Her dress fluttered thereby, the blood ebbed from her cheeks, he looked at her, and noticed how her breast rose faster, her breath streamed against him freshly.

Oh, she was perhaps the loyal helper which he sought, the sister of his poor, beloved wife, who wanted to bring him comfort.

How youthfully fresh and vigorous she was.

"Hedwig, you asked before — — —"

"About your circumstances, yes."

"I — I — Hedwig — if I just confide — —"

And then the desire to share became overpowering. He forgot who she was, he grasped her hand like that of another man, and with stammering faltering words, but also with the deep nature of this closed off soul, he revealed himself, he unburdened himself from the overly heavy pressure, he spilled all his woe out before the beautiful girl.

And truly, she was beautiful.

For while he spoke, her figure rose, her limbs seemed to stretch, to become more luscious, and while he told of the outstanding rent, of the eight days respite which the merchant in Grimmen had allowed him, of his complete breakup, it seemed then as if she drew all this hardship with greedy delight onto her shoulders to carry it from then on alone and unbowed. When Wilms had finished, he looked at her, and was frightened.

Her eyes hung to his own. In the fire of his telling, he had pressed himself to her as if he wanted to embrace her.

Horrified, awakening, he recoiled.

"There — over there is the forester's house," he now stammered.

VII

The great floor lamp was burning again in the wide living room of the leaseholder. And it had really become more comfortable already.

An ice-cold rain had set in outside, and while the time was normally spent during this transitional period freezing and shivering, now a cheerful fire was crackling in the massive tiled stove, and from time to time the agreeable sound of bursting or cracking pieces of wood could be heard.

Hedwig, laughing over the narrowness which wanted the heating to begin strictly according to when the first snow fell, had herself fed the first ample fare into the old tiled patriarch, and now the ill woman sat in a huge armchair covered in blankets, warming herself, and waited on the return of her husband and sister, who had jointly walked to the Pastor of the large village to fetch the clergyman and his family for a visit to the leaseholder's house. The forester had also wanted to come over with his wife. Hedwig had been emphatic about it, for she thought to reestablish at any price people and sociality into this desolate home.

Thus the suffering woman sat, and she often held her hand before the flickering fire until she saw her blood shimmering through her skin.

A cosy warmth streamed through her. She would almost have felt comfortable. – If she just had not remained so abandoned and alone.

Why did the pair have to go together? Hedwig alone would have sufficed. But Wilms had not wanted to let her start off in the weather unaccompanied – "it wasn't right," he had said, and now they had been away for an hour already.

The hour struck.

The invalid became ever more impatient. Maids and servants did not care for her. For the first time in a long time, work was lively in the house; the leaseholder had introduced a dairy with Hedwig's help. Today the necessary machine had arrived from Stralsund, delivered by a friend of the girl on credit, and the servants were presently getting it in working order.

Else could distinctly hear the laughing and chatting of the people.

Not even a bell was at hand for her, which she could perhaps have been able to ring.

Quite abandoned – without any external help.

She began to get scared.

Wilms could really have been back long ago. It was inconsiderate of him, and particularly for her, the pampered one, it was something completely alien.

She began moaning gently, and moved back and forth in the chair – then she held her hand before the glow again, and listened.

Outside the rain was pelting down steadily. You could seemingly hear the bubbles bursting – – but suddenly, the invalid listened tensely, a rapid, dull hoofbeat sounded in between, then something came bursting into the yard – – a horse whinnied lightly and repeatedly – a short change of voice – –

And there was a knocking on the door. Quick and energetic, and before the surprised woman could even think, a young man in jacket and riding trousers entered the room, and made a short, ingratiating bow to her on the threshold.

At the same time, his spurs clinked brightly on his tall boots, and the water dripped down from his loden jacket.

"Pardon," he began, and tugged at his cap a little bashfully – "I know it is a great liberty that I bring the entire country road in here with me. Isn't it? – I have surely found Mr Wilms at home?"

"No – no – unfortunately" – Else made vain attempts to rise – "my husband and my sister are away – but who – – with whom have I then – ?"

And again she attempted to set herself on her powerless feet, but was hindered in it by the polite and yet casual approach of the rider.

"Oh" – he thought meekly, while he shook his head constantly – "I heard you weren't well, dear woman, and now I am doubly sorry that I must frighten you so. – But this nasty weather outside – you see I was wet through, like a morel – and I thought then, Mr Wilms would surely take me in for an hour. – I am actually Count Brachwitz, the son, of course – your husband knows me quite well – perhaps you have also already heard of me – – may I take the liberty? You are too kind."

With that he drew the chair offered by Else quite close to the invalid, examined her half sympathetically, half in embarrassment, and then stretched his hand contentedly towards the massive stove's fire.

"Splendid," he uttered comfortably, and drew one of his massive top boots up onto his knee, whereby he nonetheless bowed gently to the woman of the house, "Do I really have your kind permission to wait for Mr Wilms, until he returns or the rain stops? – Or am I a nuisance to you?"

"Oh – God forbid," the ill woman coughed.

And she spoke the truth. The noble visitor who, without her really sensing it, treated her so politely and at the same time somewhat patronisingly, flattered and impressed her to the utmost. She had never paid a call on the local Count's family, and now, as though by a miracle, the young, youthfully handsome aristocrat sat before her, and was endeavouring to say all sorts of gallant things.

He listened patiently to Else's story of illness, and smiled only a little smugly when Else shared with him that she had always been healthy as a girl and her suffering had first begun in marriage.

"So? – hm" – the young Count stroked his beard, and nodded wisely, "Yes, yes, dear lady, marrying. – I am also in principle against it. If there were only some other means to ensure the right of succession, I would not think of it. I have in particular something steady in my nature. It can be seen in me, can't it? – hm" – – – he struck with his riding crop, which he still held in his hand, casually against a chair leg, and began to look around the room a little impatiently. Apparently the tete-a-tete with the invalid was beginning to bore him.

"Would the Count perhaps like to take some refreshment?"

"No – no – God forbid – don't disturb yourself, we are chatting here quite excellently. Hm – a quite cosy room – a little large – – yes – do you often sit so alone? It seems to me as if I had recently met a relative of yours at the train station. Or has she already departed again?"

"Really, the Count noticed that? No, my sister Hedwig is still here, and will certainly be staying with us for a long time."

"So? Well then I compliment you, an extraordinarily pretty young lady – so, your sister? – Well yes, the similarity is unmistakeable" – here the rider bowed again with that obliging manner which unwittingly clothed him so magnificently. – "A Miss Schröder, who resided in Stralsund some time ago now – am I right?"

"You know that as well?" the ill woman whispered, visibly flattered.

It did not occur to her that the aristocrat had turned his head back from the fire in which he had been eagerly staring so as to direct his sharp sparkling eyes for some minutes inquiringly at her hollow, pale countenance, as if he wanted to seek in it something hidden, secretive. – But then he seemed to be contented. "Yes, yes" – he continued casually, "We know each other – just superficially of course, for such delicate boarding house girls don't like to be brought together with an officer – that you can imagine."

"Oh – the Count is only jesting –"

"Absolutely not – they tell the most dreadful stories about me – – well here it will soon start too, and – –"

He interrupted himself, stood up, and listened, "Do you hear? – There outside a wagon is travelling along the main road – two steady trotters at least, now they are steering over the bridge – that may well be your husband and sister."

"Yes, probably, and they are bringing the Pastor's family with them."

"So? The Pastor's little girl has developed well since I no longer had her in my sight. Very nice. A little pale, an English tea face, but you must also make do with it."

Else rocked back and forth in her chair. A vague feeling said to her that the guest was striking a note against her which she did not suit.

"And the forester's family comes today as well," she burst out quickly, while her gleaming eyes were directed impatiently at the door through which those awaited had to enter at any moment. "I am receiving visitors today for the first time, Count – in – in a long time."

"Oh that pleases me on your behalf really quite extraordinarily," the rider suggested, and stepped slowly to the window without taking the slightest notice of the long sigh of the ill woman. "So the forester as well with his wife," he then murmured to himself, and to himself he also thought, "Strange, how my heart pounds. – I am afraid of encountering this girl again."

***

The first greetings were over. The two ladies of the Pastor's family were already placed on the massive, black leather sofa behind the huge, round table, and were darting astonished looks at Count Brachwitz from there; the clergyman himself, a small, stooped, white haired little man who did not seem to fit at all to his lean, overly tall other half, spoke bent over Else's chair those consolations which he repeated on his frequent visits with the same words almost mechanically. But even he blinked perplexed behind his glasses at the rider, as if he could not explain his presence, and Wilms stood by his noble guest in the window niche, shook his hand bashfully, and entrapped him in all sorts of farming questions, but without being able to release himself from the fearful thought of what this visit must surely signify.

Thus the first minutes of being together passed. Until the ill woman finally asked, "Where is Hedwig?" Everyone had seen the girl enter with them, but then she must have left again straightaway.

"Perhaps she is still arranging something in the kitchen," Wilms apologised. But again he had to look at young Brachwitz, who remained restive next to him.

"So? In the kitchen?" the latter commented. "Then an appearance will surely soon occur. Presumably a sturdy glass of mulled wine for the damp outside, and the famous country ham which you possess here – well don't fear, Mr Wilms, I will push off immediately, the unbidden guest will cast off."

"But you will give us the honour, and first accept a little something for yourself, Count," the invalid urged with a weak voice from her chair.

"You want thus to really to feed me up, dear lady? — Settled — then I will stay. — Well, dear Pastor, do you still think about when you confirmed me? Since then we have seldom seen each other. Miss Paula has in the meantime become a lady. — Good evening, my dear lady — incredible, I dare not act familiar anymore. Or may I still?"

Thus the nobleman said something pleasant to everyone, laughed and chatted, and had surprisingly quickly won the affections of those present.

Finally the forester's family also appeared. The forester was a herculean figure with a long, fox-red beard, booming voice, great good nature and full of war recollections. A leisurely forty year old. The forester's wife had a slender, luscious appearance with deep blue, adventurous eyes, a wonderfully white, fresh complexion, and a constant affinity for joviality. A beautiful wife who wanted to enjoy herself in naive flirting.

The chairs were placed around the table. Two maids covered it in fresh linen, Wilms pushed the ill woman's chair over, and also brought a seat over for Hedwig.

Just where might she be?

"Is the girl still in the kitchen?" he asked one of the maids in the end.

"No, sir, the young lady is up in her room."

"Wilms, then fetch her down please," Else commanded him excitedly, and fingered the edge of the table spasmodically. "Why is she holding us up so long? I don't understand it at all — the Count knows her too."

"Certainly," young Brachwitz interrupted his conversation with the forester's wife, "and it would be a real delight to me to take up our fleeting acquaintance again."

"So go," the ill woman urged excitedly.

The farmer then went out hesitantly, and climbed up the narrow stairs which led under the roof again. Next to the room which he had lived in himself since his wife's illness lay the little room in which Hedwig had been accommodated. He groped his way uncertainly in the dark corridor. Her door stood open.

It was so strangely silent in there.

Would she not be found here either?

He thus became apprehensive, a torturous fear oppressed the big man that the girl could have secretly left.

He indeed said to himself straightaway that he would not miss her, but something hidden, secretive lay here in the air which he took in.

Did he really dread her flight so much?

His heart pounded, hesitantly he stepped closer.

In the small, bare room, a candle stump was spreading some light. Dark shadows battled against the weak waves of light. The window stood open. The little flame flickered up and down in the breeze. A bed could be seen, an elegant leather suitcase, a washstand, a cupboard, two bamboo chairs, otherwise nothing. But before the window loomed the figure of the inhabitant.

She must have just washed, or cooled her skin and breasts in the water, for she was still embracing the window crosspieces with bare arms, and leaning motionless out into the cold air which could be heard drizzling dully and monotonously on the metal fittings.

Arm and neck were white and rosy as if an accursed, beautiful marble image had come to life. The leaseholder saw distinctly that her fine skin was shuddering with the chill, and yet she exposed herself motionlessly to the cold as if an immensity of fervour and defiance of life were in her.

Wilms wanted to withdraw, only he found himself rooted to the spot. Oh, how impure the image appeared to him, unfitting, distasteful, and yet he could not bring an end to his own staring, he had to constantly look, while hate, reluctance, admiration, and a distant, detested desire strayed in confusion through his straightforward nature.

Yes, Else had looked similar – at the time of his hours of happiness – but yet not so certain, so proud, so strange in her beauty.

His lips trembled.

The chill began to shake him as well as the beautiful creature in there.

Then the wind slammed the door shut. It went crashing into its lock. The entire house echoed. And Wilms staggered back, and pulled himself up.

"How startled Else will be over the bang – the poor woman," – was his first, reluctant thought, – then he waited a few more minutes, finally knocked loudly on the door and, at a surprised "come in", crossed the threshold. Hedwig was still fiddling with her black bodice, and just then doing up the last buttons. – Slowly she turned her back to him, and asked quickly over her shoulder, "Why have you come up here? Is Else perhaps turning worse again?"

"No, thank God not, I am meant to be fetching you downstairs."

"Me? – Yes, I first wanted to clean myself a little after the dirty path taken before. You see of course. – Are all our guests already gathered then?"

"Yes, they are all there. The forester too. He wants to buy the hay off me, thank God. You have achieved your intent with the wife, I thank you for that, my child. And – and von Brachwitz also finds himself down below. You probably noticed him before?"

"Yes, I saw him."

"Tell me – Hedwig – does the gentleman number amongst your friends?"

"No."

"So just a fleeting acquaintance?"

"Yes – no – that is, I know him better than that."

"Look — I don't want to interfere — it does not concern me — but — he surely courted you over there? Am I right?"

"That too."

The girl now turned slowly so that the leaseholder could look fully into her peculiarly pale countenance, and measured him inquiringly with her brown, peering eyes. "But why do you ask?" she continued slowly, "doesn't he usually visit you?"

"No — never."

"Never?"

A trembling passed over the figure of the questioner, her dark eyes burned in her pale face in suppressed, painful fervour.

Silently she stepped before a narrow mirror, pulled her askew bodice right, and brushed her brown, gleaming hair.

Wilms, who likewise had to turn his look to the mirror, saw how the young woman's full blossoming lips twitched, how her white teeth were clenched, and over her entire countenance, that smiling, defiant, wildly covetous look spread again which the leaseholder did not comprehend in his blind self-consciousness, which he brooded over, and which he detested.

"Hedwig" — — he murmured spontaneously.

"Yes, brother-in-law," she answered softly.

He stepped to the door, and turned bashfully to and fro.

"I think," he emitted hoarsely, "he comes for your sake."

Speech failed the powerful man.

Without him knowing, borderless, deep shame was seizing him so that he wanted to push himself into the girl's affairs of the heart, and yet — a consuming curiosity kept gnawing at his breast, how far had the pair's relationship prospered, whether an inner feeling could be spoken of – or whether – the blood climbed to his forehead at the same time – whether something impure, coarse was mixed in it.

"Am I right," he repeated, "he surely comes for your sake?"

"For my sake?" she repeated lost in thought.

A gust of wind suddenly swept the window. It threw the panes rattling against each other, and blew the candle stump on the washstand out so that there was complete darkness.

The leaseholder heard how Hedwig breathed deeply. Then she stepped up to him in the doorway and, as they both stepped out of the dark room, said with her accustomed resolve, "Let us leave the Count. – He is an ugly memory for me, which I would like to shake off. – By the way" – she laughed softly – "you don't need to think it was anything special, brother-in-law – a complete everyday stupidity. – –"

She interrupted herself, and complained over the thick darkness which enveloped the corridor and stairs. They groped their way arduously. Both tightly next to one another. Her dress skimmed his feet, and it seemed to him as if an agreeable warmth was streaming from her.

Then she emitted a soft cry.

On the uppermost landing of the stairs, she had missed her step, and grasped the man's arm, which he tolerated, startled. Thus they descended. Slowly as if they were indulging in deep thoughts.

Only when the oil lamp of the hallway lit up their faces dully did she turn fully to her brother-in-law, and suggest with the old, serene calm and her clear voice, "It is quite good though that von Brachwitz is visiting you for once. After all that you have told me, it will be necessary to consult with him about a reduction in the rent."

That struck Wilms like a heavy club to his forehead. – "Yes, yes," he stuttered, and bent his head dully. – His debt burden, the entire absentmindedness of his property, the ill wife in there, the bad harvest, and the high rent – all of it together suddenly caved in on him again, and lay like iron, clamped shut about his timid heart.

Hardship, worry, and illness stood again in his brick tiled hallway, ready to receive the man coming down. Up above in Hedwig's room, he had not thought of these grey guests of his at all.

Softly groaning, he let the girl stride past him, and then followed her with heavy steps.

When she opened the living room door, his weary, dragging thoughts had shifted so completely again that he thought behind Hedwig with dull astonishment about how sharply the black velvet band his sister-in-law had placed around her neck contrasted with her white skin.

"How will the two greet each other?" he pondered still, then the brightness of the illuminated room was streaming towards him.

VIII

Ha, ha, quite excellent – quite excellent," the forester Eltze cried, stretching his legs out, and pouring with bold verve new hock into his wife's glass, "Here, Anna – clink glasses with the Count – – your health, Count – quite magnificent – truly. Such a thing with training a dog has still not happened here. — Right, Anna, right, Mrs Schirmer? — Binding love letters under the dog's collar, and then having the mutt carry them into the girl's boarding house, ha, ha, ha, too funny an idea, too fu — —"

He swallowed, his face turned cherry red, and tiny Pastor Schirmer, who was sitting next to him, had to slap the giant on the back, "Dear friend, steady on," the clergyman squeaked, and sent an uneasy glance over to his wife and daughter, of whom the latter was leaning far over the table to listen to the saucily recited story of young Brachwitz with hot cheeks.

All the country goose's timidity had flown.

Even the forester's wife was following smiling the young aristocrat's anecdotes.

"My God" — it shot through the confused clergyman's trembling old head. "The women — the women — not to be unlearnt — the forester's wife and my Paula, the most pious in my parish, every Sunday in the church, and an hour of edification in addition — and now this behaviour, as soon as the first handsome, young man runs across their path."

"Ha, ha, what faces the girls must have made when the mutt arrived," the forester grunted anew, and raised a fist up high.

The country nobleman, sitting next to Else's chair, and kindly providing her from time to time with all sorts of small offices, now lit one of his own fine cigars with the permission of the lady of the house and, leaning back, tossed in between rapt and expectantly, "Well, dear Else, Miss Hedwig, — Miss Schröder," he corrected himself — "will best be able to tell us. For she found herself in this boarding house as well."

"What, that was your boarding house, Miss Hedwig?" Paula Schirmer cried animatedly in between.

And the forester cried rowdily, “Thunderbolts, our beautiful Miss Hedwig was also one of the mutt’s mademoiselles? – Well, how about that?”

“Were the company acquainted from before?” the two married women now also inquired raptly as if with one voice.

Everyone looked at Hedwig.

She had taken a seat next to Wilms and, busy with the hospitality, had taken little part in the conversation up to then.

“What will she answer now?” the leaseholder thought in his dull brooding. Pressed to the ground by his worries, and with a piercing feeling of fear in his chest, he had up to now stared at the table top, and he only occasionally looked over at his pale, strained wife, timidly and suspicious as if he had been caught in a crime.

What had only changed in his conscience?

Oh, it was only the fear, the horrible fear about his existence, the unhappy man persuaded himself.

“Nothing more – certainly – nothing more at all.”

“Were the company acquainted from before?” rang in his thoughts. – What would she answer now?

And without excitement, lofty and calm, Hedwig responded, although she looked for the first time firmly at the Count, “Oh yes – the Lieutenant often visited our boarding house’s balls. I myself once even untied one of his letters from the big dog.”

Simply, coldly, gently, she had tossed it all off, now she rose with her immaculate poise to present the Pastor a plate with cakes and fruits. She was a perfect lady.

“Please, Pastor – wouldn’t you like a gingerbread? – No? – Now then perhaps an apple, – I’ll peel it for you straightaway – allow me.”

A painful silence had occurred in the company. Even the cheeks of the ill woman, who had lain in her chair for so long impassively, turned a hectic red; with vigorous, incautious intonation, she whispered short of breath and irritably, “A letter from the Count to you? – Hedwig, that is but a jest, isn’t it? – Tell the company.”

Yes, they were all very covetous to know this. The forester’s wife, whose deep blue mermaid’s eyes radiated and sparkled with curiosity; the Pastor’s wife who sat there like a post, and found everything to a large degree immoral; and the silly, little, buxom Paula who could not expect at all to penetrate into such secrecies.

Oh, she found Hedwig to be “sweet” and “wonderful”.

But young Brachwitz did not let her answer, “A jest?” he repeated imperatively as he watched Hedwig attentively. “Yes, unfortunately it was regarded by the young ladies only as a jest, although it was damned grimly serious to me. Why wouldn’t it be? – I was young and had really fallen in love with a pair of the most beautiful boarding house girls. Are you aware, Miss Hedwig?”

Hedwig suddenly turned very pale, the leaseholder noticed how her hand spontaneously opened and closed again trembling, but outwardly she replied calmly as she turned the tap of the tea urn, “Certainly – you often made it quite clear, Count” –

“With a pair at the same time?” the Pastor’s wife echoed, repeating the Count’s words quietly and indignantly. The young gentleman’s conversation began visibly to displease everyone.

And again a long, pregnant pause set in, which no one dared to break. It was getting very uncomfortable. Else began to tremble with embarrassment. If the Count would just leave. But he remained, and began following every movement of her sister.

What did that mean?

The ill woman worked herself up so much that her teeth quietly chattered together. She noted that she was feeling feverish, but kept herself upright with the last of her strength.

Even her husband's look hung so strangely on Hedwig. It only now occurred to her.

Whether both the men knew something about the girl?

But what?

And both the married women were whispering so quietly to each other.

Over what?

It flickered before the eyes of the tormented woman, a long stabbing pain cut through her.

"God in Heaven — Hedwig," she moaned half aloud, in order to say something, "I would like — you should — sing something — I have not heard anything for so long." She shivered.

Everyone applauded. The forester, who had done too much justice to the hock, swayed to the old piano standing in the corner, and carried two candles with him, grunting. Paula Schirmer provided a stool, and Hedwig rose willingly to fetch the sheet music from the good room.

In the next room, darkness reigned.

Immediately young Brachwitz, who did not let the girl out of his sight, grasped one of the candles, and followed Hedwig gallantly with the light.

And by itself, the door fell shut behind them both.

And now the nobleman saw how the beautiful girl was standing leaning over the sheet music cabinet, and searching.

The noble lines of this youthful feminine body were proffered full and mature, the blood streamed into her cheeks, crackling golden sparks seemed to dance over her brown hair in the shimmer of the light, and Brachwitz's blood swished and roared fiercely in his veins, just as indomitably as the time when he had practised the half-crime, the boundless crudity against her.

Again he could not resist the soft, defiant magic which streamed from this woman, that silent, luscious temptation.

And the seething madness bubbling over all reason made him completely senseless.

"Hedwig," he whispered, trembling under the strain, and grasped her shoulder boldly, "Answer me finally. – Can you not forget the stupidity of that time?"

How slowly and laboriously she straightened up! And now Brachwitz noticed with fright what a transformation had come over her countenance. Rigid marble pallor was chasing away the still so resplendent redness, everything in her seemed so paralysed, so motionless, only her large eyes were directed so hatefully, and yet with flaming, inexpressibly covetous fire at her harasser so that the rider let his hand glide dazed and faltering from her shoulder.

Was it fury, was it desire which was spraying against him then?

"Dear Hedwig, if – –"

"Quiet – I don't want that –" she commanded him with a soft whisper.

"But you don't know – –"

But he broke off abruptly, and stepped back.

What was it?

With a single movement she glided up to him, stood quite close before him, her mouth distorted, her lips shook longingly as if she wanted to kiss him or bite her teeth into his flesh. Every fibre twitched and trembled in her beautiful face, and without deliberation, incoherently, throwing her hands over her eyes, she burst out, "No, you don't know – you – you don't know what you have made of me – you – –"

"What then?" Brachwitz whispered confused.

When she heard his voice, the girl started as if she had just come to consciousness of her position.

Wordless, incapable of any movement, she stared at him.

What had she just suggested? — Had she perhaps betrayed the dark, ugly secret to him which had stained and ruined her soul, her thoughts since that day? The fearfully guarded, the leprous secret which was the source of her secret fear and horror?

Hedwig felt that she would not be able to bear this wordless standing opposite each other for long, that something terrible, unforeseen must happen.

He began to smile again.

That kind, cheekily trusting smile that had made her defenceless that time.

Her breast heaved. Oh! If someone were to enter the lonely room now, or if she were able to possess enough courage to throw her harasser to the side. But nothing stirred.

And he had the audacity to immerse his eyes with their hot expression of future, certain possession in her own, a seducer who is certain of his proven power, and now he slowly set the candle down. Hedwig looked at him with astonishment.

"What will happen now?" she thought turbidly. But then — thank God, she had expected it, then finally, finally the door opened, Wilms's large figure suddenly stood next to the pair, and with warm gratitude, the girl heard how her brother-in-law said, after an unpleasant pause, uncertainly and clenched to the Count that he wanted to have a few words with him undisturbed over the conditions of the lease. The young gentleman should not be offended. — Thank God, this horrible minute was over. From then on it all happened in wild haste. Each of the three persons in the chilly room seemed to surmise the others' secrets. They spoke and contended without addressing the matter. The leaseholder asked for a reduction in his burden, the Count shrugged his shoulders grudgingly, and suggested that it was all a matter for his father. Finally they reached an agreement that the leaseholder would seek out the old estate owner personally in the following days. Perhaps Hedwig could also take on the intermediation, since the old Brachwitz was too badly attuned to Wilms.

Hedwig?

Both men fell silent as though by agreement, and looked curiously at her.

Did one want to challenge her?

"Yes, yes, I will go," she nodded half absent-mindedly, and yet pulling together her old strength.

And then Hedwig felt everything that followed as if it were through a thick haze.

How they returned again to the large room. How she then stood at the piano and, accompanied by Paula Schirmer, sung the song by Heine:

> The beautiful, sultan's daughter
> Daily walks up and down
> At evening by the fountain
> Where the white water ripples.

How it then turned so quiet around her, and a wild commotion had suddenly taken place. Else had already been sitting there for a long time trembling and robbed of all strength, and at the close of the song, she emitted senseless with effort a wailing cry, and collapsed in a faint.

Hedwig still recalled how pale and ghastly beautiful her sister's countenance had appeared to her. Timidly and hastily, the guests had then hurried away, Wilms and the girl had undressed the unconscious woman and, when she had given her first sigh again, put her to bed.

Hedwig slept this night on a sofa next to the ill woman's bed, hand in hand with her sister who held tightly to her fingers like a comfort dispensing amulet.

IX

The doctor arrived quite early the next morning. It was the county physician from Grimmen who visited the suffering woman weekly and had known the old rentier's two daughters since their childhood.

He was a small, fat, jovial gentleman marked by a misshapen belly, a weathered red, wine drinker's face, and a pert partiality for every pretty girl and woman, although he already possessed in his own family a considerable number.

Little Dr Rumpf greeted those present at his arrival with a loud, "Morning, children; well, how goes it?" stomped into the middle of the room, and remained there a while in bewilderment.

The ill woman lay as motionless and white in the bed as if she had already passed away. And her husband as well as the young girl at the head and foot of the bed seemed likewise to have already been keeping watch by the bed for many hours.

That struck the doctor alarmingly.

But when Else slowly and welcomingly stretched out her withered hand to him, Dr Rumpf pulled himself together, stepped quickly to the bed, and kissed his patient tenderly on the hand.

His prickly, white stubble scratched the poor woman at the same time so that she screwed up her face in pain.

"Worse, my child?" he asked sympathetically without paying attention to the others, "worse?" With that he unembarrassedly exposed the ill woman's chest, listened attentively, and finally shook his head.

When the physician becomes so tender, it always passes for a bad sign.

"Doctor," the prone woman breathed barely audibly, "is it very grim for me? — Tell me — tell me, please," she repeated insistently, "I am prepared for it all."

"So? prepared? yes, yes, my dear," the doctor murmured heedlessly, and moved his lips in a soliloquy. "Out," he suddenly closed his thoughts, and made an energetic motion with his head to the other two that they should leave.

Wilms and Hedwig moved into the small chilly living room with the green rep covered furniture.

Faint and sunken in herself, the girl leant on the sofa over which the grey canvas cover was still drawn, while Wilms looked out through the single window silently at the chicken run.

Since the previous evening, the two had not yet exchanged a word with each other.

A strange silence reigned between them again.

A long, fearful quarter of an hour went by.

Then the physician finally entered wide-legged, and closed the door behind him.

"Well, doctor?" Wilms asked dully, turning back at the same moment. Labouring, dammed-up fear spoke from the man's roughly chiselled features, driving his eyes goggling out of their sockets, and Hedwig shared this also. But peculiar! When she let her glance glide fleetingly over the trembling giant, a scornful pity towards this worried husband penetrated at the same time into her thoughts.

In the middle of their suspense, she smiled scornfully.

"Could you not give me a little bit of comfort?" the leaseholder stammered anew. "I cannot consider it anymore at all."

"Comfort? – hm yes." – The physician let his fat body fall heavily into an armchair, and kindheartedly stroked the hand of Hedwig who had risen.

"Well, children, always pretty outside here? I want to say something to you, dear Wilms," he then continued quite seriously, "your wife's abdominal complaint has gotten worse."

"Good God – that – that I would not have expected." The leaseholder murmured it in dull despair, and leant against the wall, struggling for breath. And after a while, he burst out, "We won't bear it, she won't, and I won't."

"Poor fellow," the physician murmured, and shook his head apprehensively, "unfortunately attacks of spasms will now set in – I thought they would long ago, long ago. And then – –"

"And then?" Hedwig interrupted him vehemently and sharply, and stepped erectly before him. "Now something energetic must happen, dear doctor. You can't let it simply continue. Don't you want to attempt an operation?"

In her vehemence, she stamped softly with her foot, and pressed her hands against each other.

"An operation?" the physician growled to himself. He shook his head, rose groaning, and began a stroll about the room. Whenever he went past the farmer, he twisted his coat buttons a little; when he skimmed past Hedwig in contrast, he nodded to her in his soliloquy thoughtlessly.

Finally he stopped and, while he contentedly rubbed his white stubbly beard, as if it had been participating majorly in the development of excellent thoughts, he gave his judgment loudly and definitely, “No, no operation; but she must go to a saltwater spa – yes, yes – quite right – and indeed immediately, for it is high time.”

“To a spa?” Wilms repeated in confusion while he passed his hand slowly over his forehead.

And the ill-fated debt occurred to him again, the unredeemed, and how almost everything was missing for him to cover even the housekeeping. The beads of sweat were appearing on his forehead, he could interject with a heavy tongue, “But – but the means for that will surely be too great?”

“Yes, it is not cheap,” Dr Rumpf suggested, and looked sympathetically at the leaseholder, “So tomorrow I will write to you about where your wife has to go.”

With that he made his farewells, grasped his cane, shook Wilms’s hand, and was wanting just then to kiss the girl’s fingertips with paternal gallantry when he drew back from her quite startled, and with a loud shout pulled from his breast pocket a letter which had been sealed many times. “I had almost forgotten this,” he chastised himself, “child, here – your father gave it to me. – There is money within, and he told me that you were already expecting it. Eh, that would have made a good story. Well? Now, adieu, children.” With that Dr Rumpf stepped wide-legged and dignified out the doors, and travelled straight to the forester’s wife, whose tender skin still displayed in the evening all sorts of signs of the scratching which the physician’s stubbly beard and his healing methods left behind every time. – – –

Both the two remained alone in the uncomfortable “good room” of the leaseholder’s house.

Both looked at each other, the farmer timidly and with pounding heart, the girl firmly and almost summoning, as if she expected her brother-in-law would like to now ask her why she had the money sent to her.

Significantly, she pressed the letter against her breast, and let her brown eyes hang encouragingly on his, but Wilms remained silent, and bit his lip firmly.

An abasement should now follow – "only no money from her – just not that," passed through his mind, and he pulled himself together, and attempted to leave.

Then a weak, rattling voice meanwhile sounded from the invalid's room.

"Wilms – Hedwig – come to me."

Both started in fright.

It sounded so distant, so ghostly.

Now it had to happen.

Before Wilms was aware, Hedwig stood straight before the farmer, and consciously, and as if there would be no objection, she pressed the letter with a firm look into his hand.

He pushed it back as if the paper between his fingers were a biting fire, but vehemently, furiously, the girl pushed the offering from her once more.

"Come to me," wailed again from within, "why are you taking so long?"

"Hedwig – what should I do with it?" Wilms stammered, indicating the letter.

"Quick! – It is 5,000 marks – a third of my inheritance – Wilms, so that you can help yourself and then pay for Else's journey, do you hear?"

"I can't – I mustn't, Hedwig."

"Why not?"

"Because – because – –" he found no answer, and just held the money away from himself as if seized by disgust.

"Is it just that you don't want to be obligated to me?"

"Yes," he groaned.

"And for what reason?"

"Because — —"

It flickered before the farmer's eyes, his throat became constricted. Oh, he felt distinctly that he must not take the money because this girl who stood so blossoming, so powerfully before him, because this beautiful strange woman had shoved herself into his thoughts, sinfully, and exciting disgust, and yet awakening something unrecognised in him which rose up tormentingly and at the same time refreshingly in him.

"And if I ask you properly about it?" Hedwig insisted simply, and laid her hand on his shoulder.

Both looked at each other for a second.

Then it happened again. It then burst out of him again. Wilms trembled all over, a thousand contradictory voices screamed confusedly in him.

"Strike her down," the one incited him.

"Have you gone without a woman for long enough?" the others whispered, "embrace her, kiss her."

"Good God, what are you turning me into, Hedwig?" he burst out mutely. "I mustn't!"

"And you don't want to help Else?" she asked anew. She had never spoken so softly to him.

A dull, dying sound came from the invalid's room.

Then Wilms suddenly pressed with a brutal giant's strength both her hands into his own which still enclosed the letter, and moved his head close to hers as if he wanted to murmur something to the girl. But no word passed over his lips, he just looked at her, and only after a space of time did it burst out piece by piece, "I will take it — if you want — for you are good — yes you are good."

It was like a secret understanding had come over the pair. And now she smiled freshly and candidly at him too, as she asked him to see to his business, for she would herself share with Else everything which had been decided over the impending journey, sparing and calmly.

He nodded, and slowly turned away. But just by the door, he stretched his hand out to her in overflowing emotion for a second time.

Hedwig was still standing and smiling.

"Just go."

"Yes, yes," Wilms murmured as though in a dream, and with a long glance, "You are good."

X

In the afternoon, the two sisters were alone. Wilms had gone into the town to pay back Mr Rosenblüt the advanced money.

It was precisely the eighth day.

And so both women had been left to themselves. The ill woman lay motionless in her bed, the Bible before her, she was fingering its cover gently, and staring out apathetically into the yard which was already veiled in semi-darkness.

Hedwig had been working until then actively and busily at her elegant silk embroidery, but now as she settled down at the window as well and propped her head on her hand, she now dreamt into the subsiding day, softly humming a melody.

The sun went to its rest dark red behind the barn. For a moment, the entire room was immersed in a magical glow, even the ill woman's countenance beamed in wonderful splendour.

"How beautiful you are, Hedwig," the prone woman murmured as her gaze met her sister, on whose golden brown hair the light was crimson as if playing in a transfiguration. And straight afterward, she whimpered, "God – I was like that too, once, and now miserable, crippled, always reliant on other people."

"Jesus Christ," she suddenly screamed in ecstatic fervour, and raised her withered hands into the radiance so that they appeared stained with blood. "Take me to you, make an end to my miserable crippling – I can't bear it any longer when I see others so beautiful, so young, and I – – oh, in the spa it won't get any better."

Hedwig did not stir.

The ill woman stared fearfully at her, and seemed to want to ask her something, but her breast just rose somewhat more spasmodically than usual.

Then old Krischan, the toothless, deaf old man crept into the room, laid with his trembling hand a sheet of newspaper on the table, and left wordlessly like he had appeared.

Since Hedwig had dwelt on the farm, a newspaper had been sent to her from the town; and hence the girl hastily rose so as to light the lamp, and be able to throw a look in the paper.

"Hedwig," the ill woman called with trembling voice in between, when the girl had already been following the day's events calmly for a few minutes by the light of the lamp. At the same time, the reader had admittedly missed how her sister had not taken her gaze off her, although she threw herself back and forth feverishly.

"Do you want to take your medicine now already?" Hedwig asked willingly as she laid the paper down.

"No, my child, not yet – I would like – sit down by me on the bed, – – If I should now go to the spa, then we will not be sitting like this anymore for a long time."

Silently Hedwig followed her sister's wish, and sat down on a basket chair which stood at the head of the bed.

The ill woman huddled with her head quite close to her sister, grasped Hedwig's hand, and laid it on her breast.

The girl felt distinctly how gasping and quick her breathing was.

She remained thus for a period, but when after a while the younger woman reached anew for the medicine bottle, Else shook her head nervously, and asked precipitantly, as if this had already lain on her soul a long time, "Hedwig, I want to ask you once, do you enjoy being with us?"

Something so fearful lay in the woman's tone that Hedwig became uneasy.

"Certainly," she responded quickly, "moreover, I only came to care for you –"

The ill woman straightened up arduously, "And what do you think – of Wilms?" she continued hastily without responding to what she had just heard.

Hedwig started. She did not herself know why. Instinctively she had to recall now the steely firmness with which Wilms had clasped her hands in the morning. Being alone with the agitated, ill woman suddenly became oppressive and eerie for the strong girl.

"Can you suffer him?" the ill woman inquired more insistently, and embraced her sister's neck in her seated position.

"Oh yes" – she murmured confusedly – "your husband makes a decent, upstanding impression. And above all things, he seems so genuinely concerned about you."

"Do you think?" the ill woman sighed with relief. – Then she squeezed her sister more feverishly so that her cheek rested on Hedwig's.

Shuddering, the younger woman felt the touch of the damp, feverishly trembling skin, a gentle reluctance crept over her when she was then kissed by the ill woman ardently and tenderly on the cheek.

"Yes, thank God," the poor woman murmured at the same time close to her sister's ear. "He still loves me. – But – but – oh God, Hedwig, I want to entrust something to you. Look, when I see you, so beautiful and healthy, just as I could be now when I imagine our happy youth, then it sometimes seems to me as if I – oh God, forgive me the sin, don't count it against me, it is only the misery speaking from me" – she whimpered in between – "Hedwig, then it seems to me sometimes as if I hate my husband, – do you hear? – who did all this to me. Bitter and venomous like I have hated no other person. And at the same time – oh, you can't understand it – at the same time, I yearn for him so, at the same time, I must always think of the first months of our marriage when I was so happy with him, and we embraced each other," she started, and opened her gleaming eyes wide.

"No – no – no – oh, you my God, all that I am saying – it is all deathly sin – Hedwig, don't believe a word of it, I am feverish – don't listen to it."

And unexpectedly she rose loudly to pray; turbidly confused, with the words of the psalms, "O Lord God of my salvation, I have cried day and night before thee.* Thou hast laid me in the lowest pit, in darkness.† Wilt thou finally shew wonders to the dead?‡ – Take pity on me – selah – selah."

After this outburst, she fell like a lifeless stone heavily and dully back onto her pillows, and remained there with slowly extinguishing eyes.

---

* Psalm 88:1.

† Psalm 88:6.

‡ Variation on Psalm 88:10.

Coldly shivering, and yet full of disgust towards this ecstatic manner, Hedwig poured into the exhausted woman, who was clenching her teeth spasmodically, a few drops of the calming medicine. Then she wiped the sweat from her forehead, which the suffering woman let all happen with the same stiffened, expressionless traits.

Almost an hour elapsed like that.

No sound stirred anymore in the large room.

Cosily dim, as ever, the tall floor lamp spread its light, and Hedwig sat on the bed and looked timidly at the woman who hated her husband as the destroyer of her health, and at the same time yearned for him in a wild, impure passion.

"Impure?"

With a weak smile, the nurse shrugged her shoulders and steered her thoughts again to herself and back to that one incident when a man had first crossed her life's path. Only, as hard as she tried, it was not the bold Count Brachwitz who appeared before her eyes — no, strangely — almost ridiculously — constantly, and more and more distinctly, the strong Wilms intruded on her, seized her by both arms, and bent down over her, ever more violently — with his honest face which could look so rough and furious. Oh, it was such a painful, miserably happy feeling. — — And she said to herself in her dreaming that everything was just the echo of Else's tale, and she imagined how warm and soft her sister had probably hung around Wilms's neck, and yet — and yet — the notion became ever more distinct until she pulled herself together shuddering, and shook herself.

Confused, she brushed her brown hair back.

The large grandfather clock struck eight times.

"So late already? — Where might Wilms be staying?" And again she was startled that she expected him.

Then — she started.

Was someone not speaking to her from the side?

"Oh, I am much better," the ill woman whispered quietly stirring, and laid her damp hand again on that of her sister, "You are also so quiet and soft, my sweet Hedwig."

The poor woman had probably lain in deep slumber for an hour from fatigue, now she rose wearily and battered, and looked around the room dully.

"Is Wilms still not back?"

"No, not yet."

"Where did he go?"

"To Grimmen."

"So?" the ill woman murmured sinking into herself – "Did he tell you that?" And after some time, she added indifferently, "He probably has a lot of trust in you?"

"Yes, I think so."

The ill woman took her medicine from Hedwig's hand, the girl fluffed up her pillows so that the suffering woman could stretch out soothed and calmer than before.

Then she lay and looked her beautiful sister in the face ceaselessly and brooding for several minutes. The blood shot into Hedwig's cheeks.

She did not herself know why.

"Do you wish for something?" she inquired hastily.

"No, no, nothing. Come, my dear, I want to ask you something – I am your sister, and you are grown-up now – you see, I would like to know now, my Hedwig, – you must not be offended though – whether you – what you experienced over there in the boarding house?"

It sounded a little anxious, but yet more insistent and curious.

Instead of an answer, Hedwig leant back deeply in her armchair, and closed her eyes. – It seemed to her as if the ceiling of the low room were sinking down deeper and deeper over her, as if she were lacking air, as if everything were too narrow and dreary on this forlorn leased farm. – Just what did her sister want with this absurd question? – How much small-mindedness lay in it. What concern of hers was all that?

"Oh, now I understand you," she finally said with her clear voice. "You are thinking of what Count Brachwitz told yesterday."

She pulled her arms behind her head at the same time, and rocked back and forth gently with the chair.

"Yes, yes," Else concurred, "it hasn't left my head at all. And that two women were involved at the same time. It all sounds so sinister, Hedwig, tell me though, my dear, what do you have to do with the Count?"

"What do I have to do with him?"

"Yes – you must understand me right – – oh, it upsets me so, and gives me so much angst – – you are still so inexperienced too – – this terrible unease has knocked me down completely since yesterday. – We both have no mother anymore, Hedwig, and here I am –"

"What do I have to do with him?"

Over the younger woman's countenance, a cold, strange smile slid, which tallied well with the ugly expression which the ill woman had chosen. Then she stretched her full figure resting in the chair, and shook her head as if she wanted thereby to cut off the conversation for once and for all.

"Hedwig, don't torture me," the ill woman cried suddenly with a pointed, irritated voice. "What do you have to do with him?"

The younger woman wanted to stand up. The conventionality of the expression pricked her directly, but the stuffiness which emanated from this emaciated woman, the dull heaviness which had already worn down the powerful Wilms, also pressed her back into her chair.

"Do you not want to give me an answer?"

"Yes," Hedwig answered.

"Now then – I beg you."

"Quite simple, Else. – The Count is, as you know, a playboy –"

"Oh God – and?"

"You heard yesterday. Hence, because he presumed there were many pretty girls there, he intruded into our boarding house, and attempted then to tie up all sorts of loose dalliances."

"But with you – Hedwig – with you?"

"With me?"

"Yes."

A quick intake of breath was audible. The gorgeous, young body of this beautiful woman turned as if it felt a painful touch, a shudder ran almost visibly over her, but then it rushed quickly and as though driven over her lips, "He attempted once to kiss me violently – nothing more."

"Nothing more?"

At first a long contented sigh of sated curiosity. Then the ill woman composed herself arduously, and looked at the slender, reclining figure of her sister with timid, astonished envy and eyes glowing with amazement.

"Yes," shot through her morbidly excited senses while she stared almost avidly at this fresh youth, "yes, she is alluringly beautiful, this elongated thing with her light brown, golden sparkling hair." And with vigorously awakening affection, she flew over the blossoming facial colour of her sister, delighted in the shrouded radiance and sparkling of her eyes, and felt how excellently the loose black dress enclosed the entire figure.

"Hedwig, my sweet child," she stammered, and unexpectedly covered the hand of the surprised woman with burning kisses. A mad, expedient hope dawned at the same time in her, "Does the Count love you so much?"

Hedwig started, and turned very pale.

Else noticed it.

"Leave it," the younger woman finally replied sourly, rose, and stepped quickly to the table to turn up the lamp.

"No?" Else cried horrified, "but for what reason?"

"He was simply impudent."

"Impudent? – Good God – Hedwig, turn around – then – then you must not meet with him here at all – if I had known that – – You did defend yourself at the time? Didn't you?"

"Yes," it flew from the table in a low voice.

It sounded as though it came from clenched lips.

"Hedwig, you should turn around. – I want to be able to see you," the ill woman cried with a penetrating voice.

And at the same moment, the girl turned, and the suffering woman, as exhausted as she was, saw in complete amazement how Hedwig, the medicine bottle in her hand, strode to the bed with her certain, self-aware expression and shrugging her shoulders.

"Hedwig, my dear," she whispered, "soothe me. Nothing further happened between you?"

"Nothing," the other woman replied, knitting her eyebrows. "Do you see that you are taking this whole stupid story much too seriously? Here drink your medicine."

"No, leave it – Hedwig – really nothing further? – Nothing further?"

Was it possible?

The ill woman swallowed, implored, begged suddenly half senselessly for a response, and lifted her haggard body up.

A pause took place.

The questioned woman stared at her. Then a scornful twitch slid anew over the curled up lips of the girl, and the answer came curt and irritated, “I beg you, give me peace now. What would have occurred then? – Come, Else, you must take your medicine.”

Thus this conversation ended. The illness again asserted its rights. It was becoming late. Every sound from the farm died away, and still Wilms had not returned home. Only when the grandfather clock had already announced the eleventh hour did both sisters hear his wagon rolling through the gateway.

“Where is Hedwig?” Wilms asked from the doorway. But he inquired in vain.

With the first noise, Hedwig had already sprung up, had kissed her sister on the forehead, and had then immediately climbed up to her room.

“Already gone to bed,” the ill woman responded faintly, and it did not occur to her that the leaseholder, looking today so fresh and happy and imposing like seldom ever, had asked first about the girl.

And look – an hour later, the happy glow had vanished from his brow.

The man sat slouched in the armchair which Hedwig had abandoned before, and listened thoughtlessly to the quick, rattling breaths of his wife. It was quite dark all around. Only a little night light swimming in oil was flickering from a glass.

And the man sat, and thought of what his poor wife had just confided to him.

“The young, devil-may-care youth had kissed her?”

It was a gross affront – for the farmer too. But he did not feel it.

He nodded, and crouched, and his heart clenched somewhat sore and raw.

“Surely she had defended herself?” he thought wearily.

In the meantime, a groan came from his wife.

He leant gently over to her, and stroked soothingly with his coarse hand over her cheeks and neck.

And at the same time, his thoughts strayed again to the young creature who was slumbering up there under the roof, just like his wife here, and who perhaps yearned and stretched out her arms longingly for her seducer.

Half numbed with tiredness, his massive head finally sank heavily onto the pillows so that Else was awakened by it, and tenderly slung an arm around his neck.

And with mad desire and extinguishing consciousness, he pressed his lips onto the emaciated arm of the pitiable woman, and groaned deeply and penetratingly in despairing soul's torment.

***

But if the desires of the unfortunate man timidly penetrated into the little loft room where he supposed the more beautiful younger woman was resting in her bed, he had thought rightly, almost as if his spiritual eye could have penetrated the walls.

There she lay, trembling with life's ardour and heart's angst, and stretching out both her white arms. But not to the seducer, no, to something else, unknown, that she could not name.

Sleep did not want to establish itself, uneasy, shivering, unaccountably to herself, she tossed about, propped her head in her soft hands, and gazed motionlessly through the little window at the starry heaven above. Over the thatched roof, the night wind was swishing close above her. She heard the eerie noise when it played with the loose thatch, and it seemed to her as if the hot, ardent voice of the young, impudent nobleman was striking her ear again. Her breast rose and fell. And then — then it rose up again — then she saw before her anew the entire image of that ill-fated hour whose details she had hidden so carefully from her sister before.

Then she found herself again in the little boarding house room, a creature paralysed by surprise and fear, being covered with kisses by the love-maddened intruder, – a creature who can only stammer out soft requests in shame, and beg for mercy, and who, after the bonds have been roughly torn from her eyes, defends herself, – defends herself with despairing, ardent, finally victorious strength against an attack by which she thinks he must rob her of something precious, most important! Good God, what has become of her since then? – What!! She throws herself down, and presses her face into the pillows. Since then she struggles thus daily. Not with the one, no, with all of them, all of them. She creeps in her thoughts up to this rough, hated one, like the hungry sea up there creeps close to the island, beats and thunders against the rocks, and wants to wrench away the stones with it to kiss them, to embrace them, and to drown them.

"Good God!" – She wants to pray. But she cannot pray. She laughs at revealed religion. She learnt that as well up there from a pair of Swedish, fellow students who had lent her all those books which chase away mist and clouds like the storm wind, but the sea of passion also whips ever more furiously in the heights.

Now it is foaming and burning. Whee, the storm whistles.

Good God – good God.

And then she throws the covers from herself so that the moon kisses her white limbs, and she cries bitterly.

Frisson of spring!

Book Two

The Burden

I

Wilms's house lies sunken in deep snow. Winter has broken early and snowed in the bleak farm completely. And yet life stirs on the forlorn property. Since the ill woman, accompanied by Hedwig, has been dwelling in the distant saltwater spa, the burdensome enchantment of the farm has relented.

Light smoke climbs from the chimney into the cold, blue air, Wilms is standing with his gumboots, the jerkin buttoned up to his neck, fresh and hale in the yard, and is having the barn repaired; the cattle and the dairy are thriving; there is activity everywhere in secluded corners — traces of future, returning abundance.

Then a sled tinkles from the country road. The barking of many dogs is heard, and then the hulking chassis stops, and unveils its strangely mixed load. It is the young Count Brachwitz and the forester Eltze going to the hunt, with the Pastor Schirmer who wants to seek out Wilms, and hence climbs out alone.

"Ho, ho — Wilms, over here — over here," the good-natured forester roars in the meantime, while he waves with his giant fists, stuck in colossal fur gloves, and all his strength, and when Wilms approaches the sled to greet the young nobleman bashfully and tersely, a large package is shoved under the leaseholder's arm by the hunter.

"Here, Wilms – from my wife. – A few sausages and the like. Well alright. – With you as a grass widower, there will be little to experience of that this time, well?"

"Yes, tell me please, dear neighbour," young Brachwitz tosses in between, reclining in his fur trimmed hunting clothes and smoking a cigar. "How is it going with your wife actually? – Good news?"

The leaseholder explains tersely that he has recently received a letter from his sister-in-law according to which the condition of the ill woman has already improved somewhat.

"Well, I congratulate you then from the heart, dear Mr Wilms," the Count responds attentively, and after he has offered the leaseholder a cigar, he inquires offhand, "Your sister-in-law will surely be returning here again shortly?"

Wilms's countenance darkens. He just nods.

"And when, may I ask?"

"That isn't decided," the farmer says sombrely, and steps a bit closer to the sled.

"So, so," the Count measures the powerful leaseholder from top to bottom, whereby he instinctively grasps his weapon, then he give the coachman smiling the sign to drive on, but not without having first expressed with great politeness the hope of being able to greet the leaseholder again soon.

"Forwards."

The sled flies away.

***

Pastor Schirmer stayed there for coffee.

In the large room in which the sickbed still stood like a dark warning, the brown drink steamed in large old

Frankish bowls on the table, and the two gentlemen sat cosily behind them, and chatted.

The farm work had been completed, the daily tasks accomplished, now the assiduous farmer could tend to his ease. Two large, long pipes, which Wilms had hidden during the years of illness unused in the cupboard, were lit, and in short time, both gentlemen, each reclining comfortably on the sofa, had spread massive blue clouds around themselves.

A sweet, pleasant aroma of tobacco filled the room.

"Yes, yes," the farmer said to himself, musing, "my poor wife could not bear the smell, it tickled her throat and I — —" it issued from his spontaneously, "liked it so."

"Dear friend, you must just defer," the little Pastor puffed, and took a gulp of coffee, "yes, must defer. In the end, our entire Christianity consists of that. — What I wanted to say — — your dear wife — — — you are surely very fearful for her?"

Wilms nodded, and continued smoking in long pulls.

Yes, he was missing something, he was yearning for something, his house often seemed so empty and joyless to him, and yet his heart constricted with fright when he thought about Else's return. His present solitary existence seemed more bearable to him then. If he could only banish this painful feeling of desire from his breast. It applied merely to his wife. Only her.

"Certainly, such constant sorrow," the little Pastor murmured with his thin voice, "it locks people to one another as though with iron chains, doesn't it?"

"Constant — sorrow," the other man repeated mechanically, and looked rigidly over to the bed. "Yes, you are right, Pastor." Both friends fell silent for a while, and indulged in their thoughts.

The pipes smouldered, snow fell outside, it was cosily warm in the room.

So they did not notice that, in the meantime, the door had quietly opened, and the fat county physician, Dr Rumpf, had entered unnoticed. In his fur coat, his fur cap, and tough waterproof boots, he looked like a bristly monster. “Evening, children, evening,” he groaned.

Hardly had Wilms delightedly robbed his cheerful guest of his shaggy envelope than the physician threw himself down puffing next to the Pastor in an armchair, simply took the mug away from the clergyman, then drank several bowls of the hot drink, and seemed to finally be warmed up.

“Damned chill,” he sniffed in the end, and slapped his round belly contentedly. “Came out here, Wilms, just to tell you that I have received a letter from the Institute’s doctor in Inowrazlaw.”

“Well, what then, doctor, what’s the news?” the farmer called with alarm and jumped up.

“Well, it’s going fairly well, he writes. You see, I said the same. Now she should still become accustomed to greater independence, and hence he is sending your sister-in-law home. On these days even. — A charming thing, by the way, little Hedwig, eh?” the physician grinned suddenly over his entire face, and scratched at his stubbly beard; “I am quite delighted that we will soon have her back again in Grimmen.”

Wilms remained standing. “In Grimmen?” he repeated dully. “Is — isn’t Hedwig returning to my father-in-law’s?”

“Well, presumably; or do you need her here, Wilms?”

“Me?”

An unease befell the strong man, he stroked his short cropped hair with his hand, then he said strikingly hard and dismissive, “No, I don’t.”

“Well, you see,” the physician said unhurriedly. Then he tapped the table with his hand. “Forwards, my gentlemen, now we'll have a game of skat; I have cards with me, and you light the lamp, Wilms."

"Dear doctor, the various card games I consider to be — — —", Pastor Schirmer wanted to object sheepishly, but the physician struck still more energetically on the table, and growled, "Oh nonsense, don't inconvenience yourself further, Pastor, — and as long as you win, your dear wife will be understanding with everything. — Who deals? — Well then — Wilms, bring the lamp — tournée, pastor? Solo too? Well then clubs. Out with the trumps, my gentlemen — Wilms, the lamp is giving off soot — what's new, Pastor?"

The gentlemen played on in the best harmony.

Only Wilms, who was usually an excellent player, committed one mistake after another, in the end he even openly disturbed the plans of his partner.

The Pastor laid his cards gently on the table.

"Now listen, Wilms" — he said seriously, "such a thing has never happened before — having the ten of clubs clear and not throwing in for me?"

"Yes, and drawing the money out of the clergyman's pocket?" the physician cried.

"What are you constantly brooding over then? You must not think too much about your wife."

About his wife? Yes, he was brooding and tormenting himself, and pondering — — but the hands with the cards were beginning to tremble with fright, it fell leaden on his heart, he was not thinking at all of his wife, all his memories referred to the younger woman, that magnificent young creature whose image he could not banish, whom he saw again and again, white and rosy, just like the time when she was revealing her young beauty to the rain. It still bewildered his senses.

And she wanted to return to her father, and not to him, not to this house that was so empty?

The gentlemen continued playing. For a few more hours, then they parted.

***

A few days elapsed, things were done assiduously, only with the dairy which Wilms had established with Hedwig, it would not go right anymore. Here the enabling, feminine hand was missing.

"If only the Miss were here again," the head maid lamented one day to the farmer.

"She has gone to her father's," Wilms thought dismally. "What are we to bother her."

Since then he had been walking about serious and reserved. The snow fell ever thicker outside and lay like a white wall about the farmstead.

Thus it again became as quiet and secluded as before.

One day after the other passed away. In the farm work, there was nothing more now to be done. The leaseholder often sat silently for hours by the window, looked across the snowed-in yard, and waited to see if the country postman would bring a sign of life from the two women.

But nothing came of it all.

And gradually he lapsed again into his dismal brooding; the large man with the short-cropped, blond hair then spent entire hours in the living room. He strode up and down, looked at the same time at the neatly covered sickbed of his wife, or took her Bible in his hand, and stared incuriously into it, as he recalled the prayers she was partial to using.

Then he began to repeat a few of the verses and occasionally shook suddenly as if something loathsome was running over him. He often also took a picture from the mirrored commode, which portrayed Else as a bride, to look at it for a long time attentively. How blond the plaits ringing her head were at the time. – How she had resembled Hedwig at that time! At such instances, he hastily placed the photograph in its place again, and ran out into the yard where he berated and quarreled with his people.

They wondered about their master. He had seldom been seen like that.

And still the desired news did not arrive.

Then finally, one morning, – Wilms was still sitting with his coffee – the deaf Krischan crept into the room, squinted at his master, and laid a letter silently on the table.

Wilms's heart pounded. With trembling fingers he broke open the letter after the old man had left, but it was just a printed form containing an invitation to a rural assembly which was being convened by old Count Brachwitz.

Wilms threw the scraps heedlessly on the floor, and sighed deeply. He was not interested in politics.

"Yes," the forester suggested, speaking to him in passing in the afternoon, when he noticed the circular. "The Count wants to be elected to parliament. He wants to found an association here for it. For the raising of morality in the countryside. Well now, old friend, it could head up quite badly for us. – The damned women – haven't you noticed it as well, Wilms? You hardly take a girl on pay for the farm work – and lo and behold, you have to sack them again. – Something is wrong with such a girl. – No – morality, – the devil knows – you can't trust the women."

He scratched behind his ears. "It happened recently too with one of the married women, – wait a moment – it was even a noblewoman near here. But don't laugh at me, I don't believe it, because too great a portion of badness belongs to the married people – disgusting, I can only say.

Wilms stared at the good-natured giant. His lips moved, but he made no reply.

"Well, good morning, Wilms, how goes it with your wife?"

"Better."

"And your sister-in-law?"

Wilms did not stir, "Over that, I know nothing."

"Well, then adieu!"

"Adieu too, Eltze."

But for a long time still, as he calculated, and wrote over his business books, it rang in his ears, "Too great a portion of badness belongs to the married people."

The sweat beaded on his forehead. The numbers began to dance before him. – If he could just find strength to fight against the wicked thoughts. But then such a treacherous idea was already gnawing and biting again. "The married people" it was – yes, but was he actually married? Did he possess a wife? – – – or hadn't God the Almighty erected a partition wall between them?

"Just not that," he groaned, "just not that. Just not these appalling, despairing accusations." And he buried himself anew in his accounts, and worked until the lamp threatened to extinguish itself.

***

The next day, he received again an identical circular. At the same time, Superintendent Grothe from Boltenhagen appeared at his place, a large, broad-shouldered man who worked on the main estate of Count Brachwitz. He was there to invite the leaseholder especially to the assembly.

"No, I'm not coming," Wilms responded, as the Superintendent shook off the snow in the large room, and the delegate cleared his throat contentedly, and opined, "You're right there too."

"Now, how so, Mr Grothe, it is actually concerns a good goal."

"Beautifully good goal," the other man roared while he twisted his mouth, "Morality – there the Count should take care of his son first. But when all the girls on the farm are made uncertain that it is a disgrace, and then such an association should be founded."

As soon as the leaseholder heard the name of the young Brachwitz, the blood climbed slowly into his temples so that he could hardly hide his discomposure from the other man. "Let it be, Grothe," he interrupted curtly, "I don't like hearing such things."

"Eh – I am not saying anything against the young man. – He's even a quite nice, agreeable man. And it is pure stupidity of the old man that he did not leave the boy in the military. Here on the farm, he naturally understands nothing and knows nothing – and commits utter foolishness. – The forester's wife cannot dispose of him either," he added softly, "but she recently had to show him the door."

Wilms could not listen any longer.

"Mr Grothe – I must now – I still have things I have to do – give my regards to the Count, and – yes, I will probably come too."

"Well wonderful," the Superintendent finished off. "Is it going well with your dear wife?"

"Yes, thank you."

They shook hands, and the Count's delegate rode slowly away from the yard.

***

But the visit had its effect.

In the long time in which Wilms had felt so lonely in the snow blown farmstead and hung with all his yearning thoughts on the distant Hedwig, he had forgotten everything that he believed he knew about her when she had appeared to him as the pure, harsh unreachably high virgin. Now, when the wild hustling of the nobleman had been described to him, the ugly doubt raised its head again, he awoke again to the reality, a vigorous feeling of contempt towards himself stirred in him, and with all his might, he sought to shake off the ugly burgeoning affection.

Ten times a day, he now read the few lines which Else could already write to him weekly, then went with his rough hand tenderly over the paper, and finally placed it in the packet in which he preserved the letters from the time of their engagement.

"My Else – she will soon now be quite healthy again – and then we will with God's help be happy again – oh so happy, like back before the difficult times began." He sighed. "If only she were here."

***

The winter progressed further and further. It headed strongly towards Christmas. Wilms noted that his people were buying little gifts for their families.

That stirred his heart. He again had to think of his distant wife.

"Should I also clean the beautiful Christmas tree for the master?" the head maid asked.

The few words sounded like sympathy as she looked at the lonely man.

Wilms thanked her.

"No, leave it, Dörthe – for me alone. – There is no point."

But in the afternoon, he had the sled harnessed, and travelled to the town. He wanted to buy Else something, to give his poor, slowly recuperating wife some joy.

He jingled down the snowy, dark country road finally into Grimmen, and chose at the town's only jeweller a little golden heart on a thin chain.

He stood by as his name, “Wilms”, was engraved into the gold.

With the poesy of simple natures, he wanted to show with it that his entire heart belonged for eternity to his wife. In the tavern at which he had left his sled, he sat for a while with a glass of grog, and chatted with the landlord in the dark brown smoke-stained bar. The leaseholder learnt that his father-in-law, the old rentier Schröder, still visited the dignitaries room every evening.

“Hedwig probably hasn’t returned yet?” the farmer inquired offhand.

The landlord with his green velvet cap answered in the negative. Then Wilms paid and set off.

It was dark and cold on the way home. The wind skimmed sharply over the open sled, and threw pointed needles of ice in the farmer’s face. A desire for a warm, cosy room crept up on him, one where a bright fire was burning, and a dear feminine hand took the thickly snowed fur from the one entering.

The air was getting more and more cutting. High above, a pair of frosty stars were flickering. Wilms was freezing. Sometimes he could see into the dismally lit rooms of the isolated detached houses as they were flying past. There he saw Christmas trees already, covered in decorations. On the main estate of Boltenhagen, church bells were ringing through the night. Dull and solemn, they rang in the celebration. Precursors of great joy.

Wilms grasped spontaneously for his breast pocket in which the little packet with the gold heart was hidden, and goaded his coachman to greater haste.

The bell sounds faded away, again snow, darkness, the country road and white fields – half paralysed with dampness and cold, the men and horses finally arrived at Wilms's house on the leased farm, and passed into the lonely yard surrounded by its thick wall of snow.

All around, everything lay veiled in darkness. Only, behind the let down blinds of the large room light was radiating.

"Nice of Dörthe," Wilms thought while he stepped down the hall, "the girl has sympathy for me."

He opened the door indifferently, started, and remained standing rigid and tall in the doorway.

II

Close before him stood Hedwig in her simple, black dress, and she stretched her hand out to him with cheerful warmth. A charming smile played around her blossoming countenance at the same time. "Well, brother-in-law," she teased softly, "does the new guest not please you?"

A flickering fire was burning in the stove, in the bright, warmed room, a dear, charming creature, ready to free the tall man of his heavy fur; everything was as he had imagined it.

But it choked the awkward man at first, as if his throat were being squeezed by an invisible hand. – Half religious ideas flew through him, like those he had nursed as a boy, or had taken up from Else.

She was here.

The temptation was here again.

All the angst he had tolerated because of her in that long period plunged into his memory and turned his greeting in-reply, when he finally pulled himself together, into an incomprehensible murmur.

"Hedwig — — welcome — you —"

Then he noticed that she was still holding her hand out to him, and he pressed it awkwardly between his fingers.

"Oh —" she twisted her mouth painfully.

Icy water was dripping from his fur onto her dress.

He apologised, and was embarrassed when she helped him with taking it off.

The table was decked out in white, a hot grog was already steaming, everything was ready for a tasty supper. Even the napkins were placed in graceful folds. You could see that this time a woman of good upbringing had seen to the table.

Wilms surveyed this layout dumbfounded.

It all came as such a surprise to him that he could not find himself in the new state. He awkwardly coerced the guest finally onto the sofa, and sat down on a chair opposite the girl.

Smiling over his embarrassment, Hedwig wanted to present a few dishes to him, but he suddenly held her already raised hand firmly, and began to fiercely question her, "Not yet — not yet — before anything, how goes it with my wife?"

The girl nodded encouragingly, "Good — absolutely surprising — so good that she will arrive here in eight days."

"What? Thank God," Wilms murmured. "Can she walk already then?"

"Yes, though still supported by a cane, but it gets better every day."

"And you, Hedwig?" he faltered, and looked blindly at her again so that she burst out laughing.

"You want to ask what I want here now actually at your place?" she finally began.

"Yes, – that is – –"

"Can you really not think of it? How ponderous you men are. – I have been sent ahead – I shall tidy up, turn everything upside down so that Else will find everything good and clean. Right, brother-in-law, does that not please you?"

"Me? Why?"

"Because you are making such a morose face about it."

"God forbid, Hedwig – you know that you are always welcome with us."

"Really?"

He lowered his eyes, and began to eat.

She, by contrast, only sipped from everything, and told him incessantly about Else, and described all the details of her stay. The half-Polish city, the institution, the doctor, the other patients, all the facilities, the baths, and the whole thing were described so prosaically and intelligibly that Wilms had long ago put down his knife and fork to listen with lively attention.

From time to time, she poured him the pleasantly warming drink, and smiled ingratiatingly when he timidly drank to her.

Nevertheless suddenly an anxiety arose between the two. Hedwig had stopped narrating, and was leaning back in the corner of the sofa, as the journey had probably tired her out. Shyness discouraged Wilms too from now suggesting something agreeable.

He looked over to her quickly several times, then observed the dying fire, folded the napkins intricately, and looked anew uneasily at the young girl.

She was dreaming as though he wasn't there; her head propped in her hand, she seemed to be thinking of something far away.

The leaseholder became restive.

"Hedwig," he cleared his throat gently.

"Yes, brother-in-law."

Immediately the girl sat up, and pressed both hands fleetingly against her temples as if she wanted to direct her entire attention to him.

"Did you not go to your father's in the town at all?"

"No, I came directly here."

"Immediately here?" Wilms repeated. A painful disgruntlement climbed up in him. Just what could she have been seeking in this deserted, snowed-in farmstead? Hastily he thought to question further, but as his look met her calm, brown eyes, he fell silent again, and scratched embarrassedly at the table.

It remained quiet for a while.

But Wilms just could not bear this calm being together. Something was tormenting and harrying him at the same time interminably.

"Hedwig," he began suddenly, overcoming himself, and for the first time, he turned his honest face completely towards her. "It must be brought up between us. It has lain too long already on my heart. — Why are you really — I — my child — I mean, why are you so good to us really?"

"Good?"

"Look, Hedwig, first you lent me a part of your inheritance, and I was able to help myself with it. That nobody else would have done for me, — no, let me — I must say it once, you also nursed my wife with whom few could last. And now — now you come back here again, to this seclusion, and want to again help and support us, and set us right, and all that I shall put up with without actually knowing why you do all that; I can't explain at all to myself, you don't seem suited to such things at all, you are like a posh, young lady, why are you thus adamant about it?"

The large man cried the last words in a vehement, almost unhappy tone.

Instead of an answer, Hedwig rose. Her cheeks had paled somewhat, but otherwise her being emanated immutably that serious calm which was peculiar to her. Slowly she stepped over to the stove, warmed her hands, then measured out the room several times with lowered head as if she were thinking, and finally stopped by the table, where she placed her fingers on the glass of the lamp so that Wilms could see the blood running through them.

Her slender figure stood close by his chair, he could see the pattern of weave in her dress.

Instinctively he turned his head away.

"You see, brother-in-law," she rose after a pregnant pause serenely and deliberately to speak, her glance always directed at her illuminated fingers, "I have also been thinking about why I wanted to return here to your seclusion."

"Want?" the leaseholder interrupted her with astonishment.

"Yes, I wanted to come," she continued more hastily, "just because it is so quiet here. – This silence is a requirement for me. – As a child, I already abhorred everything restive and noisy. But that is not the main reason," she added thinking, "I came surely mostly because of you, brother-in-law."

"Because of me?" Wilms started. But it was all spoken so dispassionately, so considered, and without a trace of tenderness, so that the leaseholder felt he must have misunderstood her words.

But the blood had shot into his eyes, he pawed impatiently with his feet, and looked at her heatedly.

"Yes, Hedwig, what do you mean by that?" he murmured.

She slowly drew her hands back from the glass, and sat down again on the sofa.

"I tell you, you have been made unhappy by our family, Wilms."

"That I am not."

"That you are though, brother-in-law. Did you not, like every other man, enter a marriage to possess a domesticity? — Now, and did you find it? — No, that was all lost to you by her illness — and even now, brother-in-law, — I must say it to you, with much pain, believe me — even now my poor sister will not be able to fetch you this happiness."

"Not be able to fetch?" Wilms echoed appalled. An icy coldness was streaming through him, like before when he was sitting on the sled.

In that moment, he hated the girl who revealed it all to him so unsparingly.

"And why not, Hedwig?" he whispered.

"Because the doctor confided to me on my departure," Hedwig concluded softly, as if she did not want to excite him anymore, "that Else must be spared just like before, and that she would never again be able to be treated like a healthy woman again, but only ever as an ill woman — you poor man."

A quiet groan interrupted her.

"See," she finished hastily, as she changed colour conspicuously, "and then it was definite with me that I could perhaps take up the function which my sister could not fulfill so that you at least did not go without too much, as you have already suffered so much."

"And then you'd want to — — ?" he stammered.

He did not comprehend it.

"Yes, I am yearning for a peaceful, steady occupation."

"But — but don't you want to marry then?" he burst out. He was ashamed when he said it.

She lowered her eyes, and shrugged her shoulders, "Hardly," she responded indifferently. "I have as the daughter of a minor official entertained the foolish wish of marrying up, but –" – she hesitated, and for the first time, became restive – "that is surely not meant to be for me. And hence someone will hardly come whom I'll please, and who is suitable for me."

"Oh Hedwig, but – but –" Wilms disagreed without thinking, – "you are beautiful and clever, it will happen." But as he said it, he suddenly had to think reluctantly that these full, red lips had already been kissed stormily and sinfully.

That ruined his evening completely.

Hedwig also fell silent. She rested in her corner of the sofa as though exhausted. – Only when he said that she was beautiful and clever, a curt, astonished look met him. Then she lowered her eyes again wearily.

Thus they sat for another hour together, and talked about everything that had been happening in the locality in the meantime. Hedwig inquired in-depth about the farm situation.

He informed her exactly about everything.

Then the clock struck ten in its case, and Hedwig rose.

Wilms sensed that he must go.

He stood up immediately.

"One more thing," he said, "here are the keys."

He took from a little basket standing on the sewing table by the window a bunch of keys, and handed it to his sister-in-law.

Heedless, the girl accepted the rattling things, and hung them on her belt, but a painful feeling crept over Wilms that Else's authority would thereby likewise be overleapt by her sister. She did not appear so beautiful to him anymore like before.

Then they offered each other their hands, and wished each other a "good night".

"Will you sleep here?" asked Wilms.

"Yes, in Else's bed."
"Well, good night."
"Good night, brother-in-law."

***

Wilms entered his loft room. On the table, a candle was burning, under it lay a large envelope bearing Else's inscription.

Hastily Wilms tore open the envelope. Inside he found a picture and a note with the few words:

> Dear good, only husband!
>
> How I would like to celebrate Christmas with you, for I am so afraid for you, but soon, soon, if God allows, I will again be with you.
>
> With a thousand devoted kisses,
>
> Your poor Else.

Wilms grasped the picture. The ill woman was sitting on an upholstered chair, her lean face with its large eyes bent a little forward. Next to her was Hedwig, slenderly upright, her full growth distinctly discernible, as if health and decline were being contrasted to each other.

The leaseholder shuddered when he saw it.

Such a confident, triumphant glow resided in the girl's countenance.

Did she rejoice that she will live and that her sister was wavering before death, Wilms thought unsettled.

It was not heated in the room. A chill ran through the lonely man from head to toe. With loathing, as if the photo portrayed Hedwig alone, he threw the picture onto the table, and sought his bed wearily and feeling shattered.

The light was soon extinguished.

III

Early in the morning when Wilms arose, he heard how his sister-in-law was already instructing the maids about something in the hall.

He looked at the clock. It was just six. And still pitch black.

He released a sigh, "Oh, if Else were still capable of that too."

A quarter of an hour later, he had barely finished dressing, Dörthe brought him coffee and breakfast. The farmer was astounded.

"Shall I breakfast up here then?" he asked.

"Yes, sir, the lady has already drunk down below."

"Well, as she wants. It's okay."

The head maid left.

Wilms sat alone for a while, and wondered at the strength of will with which Hedwig was seizing her new tasks straightaway.

Then he passed his heavy hand weakly over his forehead.

The girl constantly compelled him to engage himself with her. But he did not want to be inferior to her in industry. He had a few important pieces of business to transact nearby, and hence he wanted to ride away so that he would be able to return again towards midday.

"To be with her as little as possible," he thought.

With this resolution, he stepped to the little window, and looked down at the snow covered yard.

In a stone outbuilding, he heard many female voices speaking over each other, laughing and chatting. It was the dairy which had waited so long for Hedwig.

"Could she already be below?" he thought astonished.

When he strode across the yard somewhat later to saddle his horse in the stable, he made a detour by the outbuilding, and threw a quick look into the tiled room which was illuminated by a lamp.

Right – surrounded by her maids, he saw Hedwig standing before a large vat and lifting the large lever with her youthful strength and stamping down again. The maids murmured approvingly, and tried to imitate her with the two other vats.

She had borrowed from Dörthe a traditional work blouse on which the sleeves were missing, and now the leaseholder saw how her full arms were reddening with strain. Her breath steamed in the cold kitchen like a cloud.

That evening when he had met her alone in her room occurred again to the eavesdropper, and instantly his joy in the work happy picture was as though shooed away.

Reluctantly he murmured something to himself, then slammed the stable door loudly, and after a short time, rode out of the yard without a word.

When he turned around on the country road once more, he thought he recognised Hedwig in the door of the outbuilding watching after him.

***

“What does the master like to eat?” Hedwig asked the head maid before she left the dairy.

Dörthe pondered. Then she specified potato soup. “And the master shot a hare himself yesterday. It is still hanging.”

Hedwig was contented. She wanted to prepare everything herself. The deaf Krischan was sent into the village to the grocer for all sorts of ingredients.

He limped from the yard listlessly.

The head maid and her subordinates watched the girl admiringly as she strode busily to the house.

"She understands," Dörthe judged, "pity that the wife isn't also like that."

Over the entire morning, Hedwig cleaned up the house from cellar to loft. With Else's keys, she opened all the cupboards, counted up, and set everything right as if everything belonged to her. Her cheeks reddened with pleasure at the same time. She seemed like a housewife who had to keep man and home.

Then she took command in the kitchen. In the end, she gave Dörthe the task of having a small fir felled.

"Yes, but Miss," the maid suggested apprehensively, "the master did not want one."

"Why not?"

"He said it was because he is so alone. – And – then – our lady is also missing."

"Did he say that?"

"Yes, he said something similar surely."

The girl looked at the floor for a moment. Then she decided smiling, "I am here – listen, Dörthe, it must be a very beautiful fir. – Have we some something for decorating?"

"Now, Miss, that I don't know."

"Well, then we will make it ourselves today. – And for you too," she added. "Christian should fetch some coloured paper."

"She is too nice," the head maid said thankfully behind her.

***

Wilms noted at the table that just his favourite dishes had been chosen, and when he gave thanks in his calm manner for it, a cheerful, self-satisfied smile glided over Hedwig's beautiful face.

It offered her joy to be permitted to provide for the needs of a person, and in particular for this large, ungainly man whom fate had played so cruelly with.

They chatted amiably again over all sorts of things. The girl told of her experiences with the dairy. Wilms told her that her strength and energy amazed him. Then he reported to her about the business which he had conducted in the morning.

It occurred to him quite self-evident that he would discuss the same things with Hedwig. Yes, he thought that such good inspirations would come to him once more when she looked at him with her clever, encouraging eyes.

After lunch he led her to the stables. Hedwig advised him urgently to sell a few of the animals. The horse market was in Grimmen over the next days, and Wilms confessed that he had planned something similar himself.

Then they parted.

When the farmer appeared for coffee, he found her place empty. He asked many times after her, finally he learnt from Dörthe, who put on a secretive face, that the young woman was busy.

Wilms did not understand, and drank his coffee alone with a strange feeling.

He did not want to admit that he missed her constant readiness to be of service.

Towards supper, Hedwig appeared again, and seemed as cheerful and lighthearted as he had rarely seen her. She told all sorts of jovial stories and jokes, and often brought Wilms to laughter.

When she suggested something ribald, her face then looked so charming, around her full mouth such a fine, ingratiatingly bold look often twitched that her opposite instinctively had to laugh along.

And though this was all so foreign to the farmer at first, he soon felt so strongly charmed by it. He also possessed a sort of dry, deep humour, and it did not last long before the leaseholder responded gently to her jokes.

He nodded calmly when she teased him about his rough unhelpfulness.

Only when he lit his big pipe, and chased out of it a few massive puffs of smoke did she knit her brows.

Wilms paused. “Does it disturb you?” he asked regretfully.

He would not have liked to relinquish this pleasure. “Would she perhaps feel the same aversion towards it as my poor Else?” he thought a little put out. Only Hedwig pulled out her perfumed handkerchief, and while she fanned herself, she said airily, “You may smoke until tomorrow, dear Wilms, but no longer.”

“Until tomorrow?” Wilms thought astonished.

He did not understand her again.

Distant, long booming sounds mixed into their conversation. From the church of the main estate, which lay almost quarter of an hour away, the bells began ringing again, for the last time before the Christmas festivities.

It drew through the air like a fine, dreamy silver tone. Hedwig rose. She stepped to the window, and drew the curtain back.

Outside there was white, sparkling snow, the grey air completely filled by large snowflakes falling down slowly and heavily. The soft down seemed to want to cling sometimes in the empty space as though paralysed.

When she looked thus into the drifts, a quiet wistfulness crept up on the girl, “Tomorrow is Christmas Eve,” she said softly. Nothing stirred behind her. No answer was heard. Slowly she turned back.

Wilms was sitting at the table, his heavy head propped on his hand, and looking at the little golden heart which he had bought shortly before. A tear had rolled onto the gold, right onto his name engraved on it.

Now he looked up, “In eight days, she will be with us again,” he said softly, as if he wanted to push back his heavy emotion.

“Else?” the girl asked quickly.

“Yes. – Come, Hedwig – I want to send this heart to her for Christmas. We need to wrap it.”

The girl straightened up. Slowly she strode to the table, slowly she weighed the little heart in her hand. When she first noticed the engraved name, she looked into the good-natured eyes of her brother-in-law, who had also risen, firmly and thoughtfully.

“She will be pleased,” she said gravely and emphatically.

The little box was laced up, Wilms wrote the address, Hedwig brought the candle and sealing wax to him. He pressed his signet into it.

With a strangely rigid look, she followed his actions. A drop of the liquid sealing wax fell on her hand, and lay on the white surface like a round drop of blood.

“Oh” – Wilms cried shocked, “I’ve hurt you.”

“Me?”

She had hardly noticed anything.

“It isn’t burning anymore,” she calmed the farmer, fending him away.

Straight afterward, she nodded affectionately to him, and walked to the door. – At the same time, she surely did not see that he had stretched his hand out to her as he always did when he said “good night” to her.

The door closed before she could notice his wish. Estranged, the leaseholder watched after her. Then he walked up and down the large room for a long time until he finally stood under the window, exactly where Hedwig had stood before.

And just then, like her, he peered into the soundless driving of the snow, he pressed his forehead on the icy glass, and did not stir. Was he thinking of his distant wife?

He was imagining how she would sling the golden heart around her white, emaciated neck, but as he pictured it, the flurry outside became more and more stormy, the snowflakes whirled and scrimmaged more and more furiously — it confused his thoughts.

"What would Hedwig probably say," something muttered in him, "if tomorrow I were to lay the thin chain around her neck?" He wanted to shake off the thoughts, but in his imagination, he bowed, and kissed her on her white, blossoming neck. And his imagination brewed more and more ardently and furiously. "If she were then to sling her arms around him, and raise her red mouth to him, like a loving wife who nestles against her husband?"

A mad smile played around his lips.

Suddenly he started, and broke out into a violent, painful groan, "Jesus Christ — not into temptation," he stammered, "oh God, not into temptation."

He folded his hands as though in spasms.

And outside, the bells were still ringing, bim — bum — bim — bum, solemnly soft, like the song of admonishing spirits bearing the message of the saviour even into this isolated farmstead buried in the snow.

IV

Thus Christmas festivities had arrived. Early in the afternoon, Hedwig asked the leaseholder if he would like to leave the large living room. Something secret was being prepared.

Grumpy and petulant, like he had never behaved towards the girl before, Wilms thereupon went out of the room without a word and, at the same time, avoided looking at her. But in the midst of the preparations for Christmas Eve, this behaviour did not seem odd to Hedwig, she called her faithful Dörthe, and worked with her behind locked doors.

Meanwhile, Wilms sat in his room, and wrote a letter to Else. He appealed ardently and insistently to his wife to return as soon as her health would somehow permit it. He delighted over her return as though over a festivity. Everywhere he was missing her. Everything reminded him of her. Oh, if she were just there. – Right at the end, he also mentioned Hedwig. She was running the household to his satisfaction, but she could naturally not replace his poor, beloved wife. He faltered when he wrote it. His blood swished and hummed through all his veins. "Lies – lies," it sounded distinctly to his ears. Hastily he concluded his writing, and then sat for hours in the ever darkening room.

He knew that Hedwig was decorating a Christmas tree down below. For his people of course, he sought to convince himself. But all the same. Soon she would send for him so that he would take part in the general, great joy. "And he would then stand with her together under the flickering candles?" he brooded, "and then be alone with the girl while the tree spread its powerful aroma of fir, and the little flames licked bright and erect at it?

Would the tantalising thoughts not then return, the thoughts which had tormented him yesterday into madness? – No, no – just not that anymore. – How would it be if he crept quietly out of the house, and spent the evening somewhere else, perhaps with the Pastor?"

He rose as though hunted, threw his coat on, and tiptoed gently down the dark stairs.

He crossed the hall, then the door of the large room opened, a figure stepped out.

Wilms started, and instinctively stopped. The darkness hindered recognition.

Hedwig uncertainly approached the silent man.

"Do you want to go out, brother-in-law?"

"Yes."

"Now?"

"Yes, I have a necessary errand still."

"But not now," the girl insisted, and seized his coat lightly. "I wanted to fetch you right away; Wilms, you won't leave us alone on Christmas Eve?"

The leaseholder turned back and forth, the more she begged him, the more agonisingly he thought himself tortured, "It all gives me no pleasure though, Hedwig," he burst out. "It torments me honestly."

"Oh – no, no," she disagreed, and grasped his hand.

That confused him even more violently.

"Hedwig, I can't watch anymore when others are delighted, and I alone shall be excluded from it. Let me rather leave, my child, I want –"

But she still held him. Her hand lay firmly in his own.

"You are much too good for that," she said softly and pityingly like a person seldom speaks to the unhappy. "Do you want to rob me too of the entire pleasure?"

"You too?"

"Yes naturally – we have decorated the tree for you." Her hand still rested in his, but with the other hand, she now hastily flung the door open.

A broad, radiant light fell into the dark hall, and poured its radiance over the pair standing close together.

Large, dark green, with wide reaching branches, the fir tree stood in the middle of the room, colourful paper chains wreathed from branch to branch, countless wax candles flickering, and behind it the staff of the farmstead, men and women, all dressed in their Sunday best, were waiting for the master of the house to open the festivities with them. Right in front of the tree, however, Hedwig had positioned two little girls, children belonging to the staff. They were holding red paper roses in their hands, and sang with weak voices a little song which closed with the words:

Joy on earth and peace to all men.

When they had sung that and Wilms looked into the radiant light and into the expectantly festive faces of his people, he did not pause any longer, he slowly placed his hands over his eyes, and cried bitterly.

And the staff nodded to one another, and prodded themselves furtively, as they knew what was oppressing their master.

But Wilms only let himself be overwhelmed for a few seconds. Then he straightened up, and looked at the girl who had arranged everything just for him. The light flooded over her brown hair, her large eyes hung firmly and questioningly on his own. She still stood close next to him.

"Thank you, Hedwig," he said simply, and squeezed her hand with desperate fervour. "We have never ever celebrated Christmas so beautifully in my house." He let her step ahead, and then followed her into the room.

The leaseholder sat joyously excited afterwards in his corner of the sofa, and followed Hedwig as she offered each of the staff a little gift of money which Wilms had specified for his people, and added in addition something special for themselves. Dörthe received a petticoat, old Krischan a tobacco pouch, Hedwig kissed both small girls and bound silk scarves around them.

Thereupon general bowing and handshaking.

"Thank you too, sir – many thanks too, Miss – no it is far too much – such a thing I couldn't accept – Lord and how beautiful the linen is."

With that the people left, and Hedwig went with them.

The leaseholder again sat alone, and looked dreamily into the calmly burning candles.

Then the door flew open once more, "From Santa," was called out and then twice more, "From Santa – from Santa."

Three packages clattered into the room, and since only Hedwig could call out so freshly and brightly, the farmer knew that the three presents were meant for him. He waited to see if Hedwig would not return again, but when he remained alone, he opened the packages. In the first, he found a carton of fine cigars, then a meerschaum mouthpiece, in the last finally a leather picture frame on which a wreath of blue violets had been embroidered in silk. A note was fastened to it with a pin, and on it was "from Else".

Was it possible?

The farmer carefully took the frame in his hand. And his poor wife was supposed to have produced this wonderful gleaming wreath with her trembling fingers? A doubt crept over him.

But who else?

Behind him someone approached, a soft rustling became audible, Wilms turned around, and looked into the gentle face of Hedwig.

He raised the embroidery up, and asked excitedly, “Really from Else?”

A shadow flew over the girl’s brow, but she affirmed it. Only the disbeliever was not convinced.

“Hedwig – I don’t believe it – Else never learnt such fine work at all – did she – Hedwig – from you?”

Again she shook her head gently.

“Just say it,” he cried insistently.

Finally she admitted it, “Well yes, it is from me,” she confessed, “Else wanted to make something like it for you, but she isn’t capable of it yet. So I took it over.”

“So also from you?” the leaseholder murmured with trembling voice. He stood a while sunken in thought under the radiant tree; without speaking a word of thanks. “And I,” he pondered to himself, “I did not think at all of preparing this dear, charming creature a little delight. With empty hands, I stand before her as if she did not belong at all in my house! Whilst she –”

It ran over him hot and cold. He did not dare at all to raise his eyes for shame. Slowly and apprehensively, it forced itself over his lips.

“And the cigars and the mouthpiece, Hedwig, from whom are they?”

From her eyes, a mischievous spark flickered; around her mouth, an impish trait flew. – The strange unhelpfulness of the man enthralled her.

“From whom are they? – Who knows?”

She shrugged her shoulders, but when his disturbed countenance enlightened her that he was fretting and suffering, she was sorry to have injured this reserved nature whose deep mood lured her ever stronger and more vigorously.

The candles were still burning, it was so comfortable in the room, deep silence surrounded them both.

Wilms started. He had not noticed in his brooding how the beautiful girl, after she had waited a long time for a word of thanks, had turned away disappointed, and sat down at the piano.

She now played. An old nursery rhyme which she varied and cycled rang out quite gently under her fingers.

"Sleep, child, sleep."

The farmer listened attentively. How gentle it sounded, like when a mother rocks her restless child. Yes, and his mother had also sung the same to him. A poor fisherman's wife in the cottage by the shore. Oh he yearned so for calm, his heart was weary, and he wanted to sleep as dreamlessly as when he had been in his mother's lap.

Hedwig played more and more seriously and vigorously. All the notes clamoured the old song, like a choir was now singing it.

The leaseholder shivered, instinctively his look fell on a simple silver ring which he had taken from the finger of his dying mother and worn since on his watch chain. He furtively kissed the ring, and stepped behind Hedwig's chair.

And the roaring and thundering eased, the powerful tones petered out into the distance ringing out like a sweet, stammered child's greeting.

She was still playing the last dying notes, when she felt how Wilms laid his hand on her head and stroked her hair softly. – Gently, gently, a shy, timid caress.

The playing immediately broke off, but she did not lift her long lashes.

Once more he passed softly over her plaits, then – her heart faltered – then she felt how her hand was grasped, and a silver ring was gently placed on her finger.

"There, Hedwig," he spoke softly, "you played so beautifully — I give it to you — it is from my mother."

She started spasmodically, looked with her brown, serious eyes up at him, and wanted to respond somehow, but her tongue was as though paralysed. Only a dark red glow climbed slowly over her neck and cheeks.

Then suddenly his hand, which still rested caressingly on her hair, became pressing and heavy as if it had transformed into iron.

Hedwig would have liked to have cried out, it hurt so much.

"What is with you, brother-in-law"

Oh, it only stood for a trivial thing, almost nothing at all; it was just eerie to see the protruding eyes which stared fixedly at the bed. Quite accidentally, the leaseholder's look glided over the neatly covered bed, and then, — just then his hand became as heavy as it if had become iron.

In the bed lay Else, shadowy, emaciated, pale and stretching her arm out to her husband who was caressing her sister.

"Wilms," Hedwig cried in horror, and sprang up. Her powerful voice shooed away the ghost.

"Yes, yes — Hedwig — do you want something?"

"For God's sake, brother-in-law — what is it with you? — are you feeling ill?"

"No — me? God forbid — it just seemed to me so — strange. — I think — it is ridiculous — it seemed to me as if Else were lying for a moment over there in your bed," he murmured simply, and yet with inner horror breaking forth.

"Else?" the girl stammered.

Both stared at each other, both tried to force a smile, but they were shaken by fear as if a cold, grey ghost were standing between them.

It was the first time that it had driven them apart.

The farmer stirred first. “We shall call it an end for today,” he pulled himself together quickly – “it is already late – good night, my child.”

They offered each other their hands as always. The girl’s fingers were ice cold. Then Wilms stepped to the tree, and extinguished the candles.

It became darker and darker, Hedwig watched indifferently as one flame after the other died under his fingers, until finally only the candles on both sides of the piano still burned.

“Good night,” Wilms murmured once more, then he hastily left the room.

It seemed to Hedwig as if she must hurry after him, throw herself in his arms, and seek protection, help against the dream figure there in the bed which would now also capture her.

If she then also noticed the phantom, if it lay next to her and embraced her with thin, white arms in order to strangle her!

“Why?”

“Because you desire the same man that belongs to me – to me.”

Hedwig emitted a quiet cry of fear.

“Give me the ring,” it wailed on next to her. “It is not owed to you!”

“Light – light.”

With trembling hands, Hedwig lit the tall floor lamp, and looked around. All around, everything lay peaceful and still, everything immersed in the sombre light of the lamp. Now Hedwig smiled, and sat at the table, but it was a weary, heart-rending smile, and when the girl felt the ring on her finger, it seemed to her as if if were pricking her.

"White silver means tears, the people say," she thought.

Worn down, she stepped again to the piano, and let her fingers hurry once more over the keys. The notes penetrated softly through the house, and to Wilms, who up above in his bed had pressed his head against the wall, and begged for slumber — it was suddenly caressing around him, the dear, old melody, the song which his mother had sung to him, "Sleep, child, sleep."

But it had lost its magic effect. He did not find peace anymore, but thought unceasingly of the wonderful, beautiful woman to whom he had gifted the silver ring.

Thus Christmas Eve ended in Wilms's house.

V

Come, Hedwig — don't you want to go to church with me?" the leaseholder asked the next morning as he stepped in his Sunday coat, the prayer book under his arm, into the living room where Hedwig was sitting before the window and reading.

The questioned woman looked up. She looked tense and pale today, and even the leaseholder displeased her in his long, black frock coat. The garb made him seem old Frankish, bourgeois. — Before, in the boarding house, Hedwig would have laughed over such a figure.

Just what had become of her?

"Good morning, Hedwig, won't you accompany me to church?" the farmer repeated more insistently. To him the walk to church at Christmas seemed self-evident.

Hedwig remained silent, turned the ring which he had gifted her the day before, and then declined his request with curt words.

"You don't want to?" Wilms stuttered as if he could not believe it.

The girl tapped her book, and shook her head. "Just go alone, brother-in-law. It is too full for me in the church. The number of people there disturbs me."

"Disturbs you?"

"I can't recite any of the prescribed prayers either, you know, the God in whom I believe does not care for singing at all."

The leaseholder stared blindly with wide-open eyes at her. A deep sadness drew gradually across his honest face. — She was so beautiful when she spoke so vehemently, the small full mouth twitched so defiantly at the same time. The farmer sighed heavily, and replied with a low voice, "I brought you my wife's prayer book — — I didn't know that you — that you are of that mind — — and so —" he turned the little book back and forth, "you won't accompany me then?"

So much melancholy was expressed in the request that Hedwig's heart instinctively beat faster. But a look at the patriarchal frock coat and the well thumbed prayer book brought her around again.

Her vehemently burning disposition came over her suddenly like a dream. She yearned for love, for storm and defiance towards the man, for something which she did not yet know, — and now this black clothed, unhelpful man with his atmosphere of dull church air.

She seemingly awoke. The hour in the boarding house room occurred to her, — and — —

"No, I won't go," she decided resolutely.

Wilms nodded, and let his blue eyes rest once more fully on her. "As you want. – Then rest here, Hedwig. And when I return, you can sing again as beautifully as yesterday."

He could not perceive her blushing anymore, even less the vigorous movement as if she thereby wanted to hold it back.

Slowly he stepped across the yard into the clear winter's day, while the girl watched after him through the window, serious and sombre.

In the church of Boltenhagen, on the high oak pews, a place remained free next to Wilms. Here Else had sat previously, and the leaseholder had envisioned nicely seeing this space taken today on the high festive day by Hedwig.

Her voice, which had stirred his heart yesterday evening, would have surely sounded silvery bright if they had both followed the psalms together from the little book, head to head. And now – – – the organ roared, the congregation gave voice, but Wilms's lips moved only mechanically, he was thinking constantly of the beautiful, young creature at home who found no joy in the Christian faith.

He wondered why he could not be impatient with her, why a still higher partition wall did not erect itself between the faithful man and her, the godless woman – but strangely, today the service of the Lord did not edify him either, he found no solace in the words of the little Pastor Schirmer, again and again his thoughts occupied themselves with the girl, he felt a vigorous desire for her, and did not understand why he had not remained with her. And yet the organ roared so imperatively, and yet the birth of the Lord was being celebrated.

He was horrified. He was already thinking entirely with her thoughts. He also possessed no God anymore, only a woman that he wanted to embrace and kiss, and kiss again and again, his saviour was a girl who was enticing him away, away to lust and life and work.

"Throw the burden from yourself," it twitched through his mind.

Had the Pastor spoken it? – Was it a Bible text? – He did not know.

***

When Wilms had left his sister-in-law, Hedwig had remained sitting motionless at the window for some time. Sometimes she looked at the thin, silver ring on her finger, sometimes she looked astonished around the wide room, as if she did not comprehend at all who had moved her there. Everything was suddenly too narrow and dull for her. The appalling fear from the day before still pressed on her nature, it darkened it as if she had been cocooned up to now by an evil enchanted sleep.

"Air – light."

She peered down at herself. The simple, black dress appeared poor to her.

Just what had happened to her in the meantime? Outside the countryside shone and sparkled. – The thickly snowed trees on the road looked like enormous, white corals.

The girl was struck by a fierce, hot urge to storm out there, to tumble about, to activate her fresh, swelling strength. Yes, she wanted to celebrate as well. There was a small tiny sled in the house. To steer it herself, and then fly on the smooth path, that would make her sound again.

Barely thinking, she had slipped into her narrow, dress-like, fur jacket, had put on her pert beret, and was now running across the lonely, deserted yard.

"I think I am quite alone in this pious house."

But she was mistaken.

Old Krischan, the sorcerer of the farm, was sitting before the stables, and trembling from the chill or from frailty. Next to him, the raven was keeping his constant sleep and trembling as well.

This pair had been odious to Hedwig from the beginning.

"Old man," she commanded, "fetch me the sled from the stables and the brown horse with it."

The old man awoke from his slumber, and grinned at her.

"Does the Miss want to drive off?" he coughed.

"Yes, and quick now."

Only the old man had not heard, or did not want to carry out the order. Slowly he crept to the side, and shook his head.

The girl looked at him, "What does that mean? Didn't you understand me?"

The old man shook again, and stuck his hands in his trouser pockets. Then he began to tremble anew, like a skeleton clattering in the wind.

A despicable sight.

The blood climbed into Hedwig's face, she stepped close up to the ugly old man, and said sharply and firmly, "Christian, it is time that you left the farm and went to the parish hall. — Do you understand? You can manage nothing more here, but there you can relax. — My brother-in-law will provide food for you. Do you want that?"

The old man had understood exactly. He trembled, kept chewing, and murmured calmly, "I'm staying here. You are not the lady of the house. You have nothing to say here."

"What?" Hedwig responded, blanching, "that will be found out." With quick breath, she entered the stables, where she found a farm boy leaning his flax blond head on the manger, and sleeping. She called to him, and with his help, the small, blue sled was soon lifted out and harnessed to the beautiful brown horse.

Hedwig sat herself in it.

“But the coachman is at church,” the boy said.

“No problem — I’ll travel alone — adieu!”

She cracked the whip; the brown, a racehorse with half-English blood, made a sideways leap, and flew with her out of the yard.

Quick as the wind, it went over the white country road. The little sled bells rang and chimed, all around there was not a human soul to be spied, everyone had attended church, only she, she alone, now enjoyed the white, sparkling landscape.

How her cheeks reddened, how her eyes sparkled with delight and joy. The past, dull weeks were forgotten, it was the Hedwig from before again.

When she glided past the church of Boltenhagen, the believers were just coming out, the entire square teemed with festively dressed men and women. It seemed to her too, as if she had recognised her brother-in-law standing on the portal steps in his long, black coat and his fluffy top hat and looking over at the team.

Whee! A new crack hit the brown so that the small vehicle shot past like a thought. She wanted to be alone for once, forget everything, shake off everything.

“Was it her? — Was it not her?” Wilms thought, and strained his eyes to the utmost. “No, she promised to wait for me,” he comforted himself then. The desire from before grasped him more and more vehemently. He struck out powerfully in order to get home.

Meanwhile Hedwig had arrived in open country. Like an enormous, rigid sea, it stretched out on both sides of the main road, the bordering bush, and the little ice-frosted fir saplings seemed to be enormous breakers which had been fixed by a spell at their height. The wind only drove off light flakes of foam sometimes.

Breathing out deeply, Hedwig travelled into it, and now grudged her steaming brown greater rest. And step by step, sometimes with loud whinnying, the animal drew the sled through the deep snow, for probably two miles until it had reached a tiny tavern lying on the country road, which was named locally the "Flagon".

Here the girl threw a blanket over the brown, climbed down, and entered the low, whitewashed bar. A colossal tile stove was spreading an enormous heat there. A dry, scrubbed white, pine table stood before the window, a few heavy chairs before it, otherwise only a black leather sofa shining with fat, and several prints of oil paintings portraying happy family scenes formed the furniture of the deserted bar.

And it remained desolate for a while yet. If an invisible bell had not sounded brightly at Hedwig's arrival, the Flagon's landlady would have known nothing at all of her visit.

But after some time, a little, pale woman appeared, two children clasping firmly onto her skirt while a third, an infant, was carried on her arm; and she promised at Hedwig's request to bring a glass of milk.

Hedwig sat down at the white scrubbed table, pulled off her gloves, and looked through the small, paper patched window of the bar across at the sparkling fields.

Outside, her brown was standing. It shook itself and whinnied loudly.

That gave her thoughts the direction.

"It would be best," she deliberated, "if I climbed onto the sled again, and then went quickly, far from here into the town and further again from here, much further, where I would hear nothing more of all that which I left behind here. Oh, it would be so good if I now left, before – yes, before something bad happened. For it will happen. I don't know why, but it is all so unhealthy in

Wilms's house, so infectious, I wish I had not returned there. — Why did that occur to me only today?"

She propped her head in both her hands, and sat for a while motionless. The iron plate in front of the stove cracked, and bent back and forth regularly. Arguing voices echoed through the corridor. Behind in the yard of the house, several men were speaking with one another.

The girl stirred. So she was not alone here? The landlady of the Flagon also had not brought what she asked for yet. She became impatient. Finally the pale woman appeared again, and placed a pint of fresh milk down before her guest. Hedwig inquired whether other guests were being hosted.

"No, Miss, my husband just has visitors. We want to sell a horse."

With that she went out again.

But while Hedwig was sipping on the glass, outside the hall door was opened again, and the girl heard a powerful man's voice speaking.

She grasped her gloves and listened. Only she could not hear any more. The loud conversation had petered away again. Nevertheless she had been gripped by a strange unease. She wanted to set off. She strode quickly to the door, and called the landlady, who also appeared promptly with her infant in her arm, and wiped the table clean with a cloth.

"Now, is that horse already sold?" Hedwig asked.

"Yes, they have already agreed."

"Who is the buyer then?"

"Eh, I don't know him. My husband addressed him as 'Count'."

"Count?" the other woman stuttered, blanching, "perhaps Count Brachwitz?"

"Yes, he might have been called that," the landlady answered indifferently, and dried her hands to accept the payment.

"Here, dear woman, here you go — — here you go." Hedwig's movements became hastier and hastier. In vain she burrowed through her pockets, but without being able to find her purse. She had probably forgotten it entirely with her hurried departure to take money with her.

"Well, that's no problem," the landlady of the Flagon consoled, surprised, "the Miss will send it to me then."

"Yes, yes, I will send it to you."

Just putting on the beret which she had taken off, and she could hurry off. With hasty fingers, she set it right, then steps echoed along the hall, and at the same time, Hedwig looked through the window as the landlord of the Flagon lead a saddled riding horse close by her sled.

Now the girl just hoped that the man whom the stallion out there belonged to would go past the closed door of the bar. But fate decided otherwise. The door opened, a slender man in grey jerkin and fur cap looked in, and called good-naturedly, "Landlady, I have added a few talers — we are now agreed. But woe to you if it really isn't a bag of whalebones. — Well, good — — —"

"Morning," he wanted to say, meanwhile in the midst of his words, his glance fell on the lady who had turned her back to him beforehand, whose figure however seemed so singular to him that he immediately recognised her. Then he too blanched, and lost control over himself. All sorts of resolutions passed wildly through him. Should he not rather simply set off? Or did he want to endeavour once more to approach the beautiful girl whom he had so offended?

What if she now showed him the door in front of the landlady?

He stared uncertainly at her, and noticed that a tremor was running over her averted figure, as if she were also struggling with herself. Suddenly she turned around hastily. “As I said, I have forgotten my purse — yes, I — I will send the money though, dear woman,” she burst out bewilderedly in order just to say something, and she stepped quickly to the door on whose threshold her oppressor from before still remained.

She did not look up. But in her entire manner, so much defiance, strength, and self-awareness was expressed, and she was in her bewilderment so peculiarly beautiful, that Brachwitz stepped back completely overwhelmed, and tore his cap from his head.

“Good morning,” he murmured with a respectful bow as she strode past him.

She nodded imperceptibly, and then flew out onto the country road. There the landlord of the Flagon had slung a feeding trough on her brown, and was now holding the black horse of his noble guest so that he could not be of help to the girl in freeing her animal from the hanging tin again.

She stamped her feet with impatience, in her rush she did everything over-hastily. Even the blanket she could not fold together quickly enough.

She would have liked most of all to have run away on foot through the snow.

The young Count Brachwitz meanwhile stood on the low steps of the tavern, and observed the girl’s endeavours raptly for a while. Then he stroked his moustache scowling. He was honestly sorry that Hedwig had such a bad opinion of him, and he cursed his impulsive blood which had driven him that time to the blatant offense against her. Decisively he sprang to Hedwig’s brown, took the trough from the animal undeterred by her backing away, then he folded the blanket, and stepped politely to the sled which Hedwig had meanwhile boarded helplessly.

"May I lay the blanket in here?" he murmured softly.

She nodded, and turned away as he threw the woolen blanket gently over her feet.

"No coachman?" he then asked with astonishment as he put the reins in her hands.

"No," she responded firmly, "I drive it myself."

She lifted the whip.

Only before the brown drew away, Brachwitz had stepped onto the sled's runner. "I would like to ask you – gracious young lady, to hand over the reins to me," he asked softly, and in a daze.

The tone was honest, the salutation respectful.

Hedwig turned her large, brown eyes to the handsome man. Her look was odd. It seemed as if she wanted to read his entire being. And after a short time, she said curtly and drily, but with trembling voice, "Step down from there, Mr von Brachwitz, I must definitely decline your accompaniment. – Once and for all."

"Once and for all?" he repeated.

"Forwards!"

Again she raised the whip, but the Count's hand was placed gently on the handle.

Hedwig started, and straightened up, breathing heavily.

"Dear young lady," he asked insistently, "I beg you – beg you from the heart – listen to me for just a few minutes. You do not know at all how much it means to me to – – well yes, to justify myself to you. May I not then, if you will not tolerate me with you in the sled, at least walk alongside, naturally only so long as it pleases you to travel slowly? – I would like very much to receive your forgiveness, may I?"

He grasped the reins of his horse, and since Hedwig made no answer, he took it as agreement, and was not ashamed to stride along by foot next to the slowly gliding sled, and to lead his animal with him.

It seemed to Hedwig herself as a sort of walk of penitence, as if the young man who had so offended her wanted to humble himself alone. She looked at him with interest. But at the same moment, it occurred to her how ardently and madly this strange man had already kissed her once. That suddenly outraged her again so furiously that she decided to bring the scene to an end.

"What do you want from me?" she inquired harshly.

"To finally obtain your forgiveness," the Count replied ingenuously. – "I feel absolutely ashamed that I acted towards you so nastily; Miss Hedwig – gracious young lady, will you not give me the assurance that you won't be angry with me anymore?"

"Yes, that I will. But under the condition that our intercourse is thus at an end, and our ways will never cross again."

"Never again?"

"Correct."

"And why not?"

"That you know anyway – because it would be pointless, Count."

His dark face coloured more, he looked at her fully, and sensed again her beauty. He gently sighed, and placed one hand on the back of the sled.

"You are right," he finally admitted in response, and over his fresh, open features lay a shadow. "Oh, nonsense, Miss Hedwig, I must tell you at once, we honestly want to deal with each other. It is actually pointless. Although I was really good to you – no, you won't get angry with me, to you I was really good, if I also mistreated you at the same time in my madness, I underestimated you perhaps – – but that alone is not it –"

"Well, but?" the girl asked hastily. Her heart was pounding. It suddenly flashed in her as if this young aristocrat who was unburdening his love to her just then so ingenuously were stretching his hands out to preserve her from a fall which she expected. "Well, but?" came trembling over her lips. "What do you want to still share with me?"

She knew now, she did not love him, but she wanted to be saved.

"But," he murmured reluctantly, and pulled on the reins of his horse – "I got engaged the past week in the capital."

"You?"

She said it almost in horror. All the blood drained from her cheeks. And yet it only thus shivered through her so coldly because she now considered herself destined by fate for a downfall.

"And who is your fiance?" she tried to stammer, but at the same moment, she had struck her brown with the full force of the whip, the animal started up, and then raced in full fury with the sled along the snow covered main road. She barely heard even what her surprised companion called after her.

With all her strength, she pulled, and tugged at the reins, but she had completely lost control over the foaming animal. Like rushing dream images, trees, houses, and people shot past her, the air swishing past took her breath.

***

In the farmhouse, the farmer had not found the woman he sought. He asked old Krischan. He shrugged his shoulders, and pointed to the country road.

"She went away there, Krischan?" Wilms inquired with concern – "alone? Did she not sit in the sled?"

The old man nodded, and kept shivering.

"Away?" Wilms murmured as he strode back to the house. And he had looked forward to being together with her. The lonely big room seemed inhospitable without her. When the girl had not returned after an hour, he threw himself in his usual jacket, untied the farm dog, and wandered along the country road to Boltenhagen.

In the hard snow, the sled tracks she had left could still be seen. Wilms's heart constricted. Since he already was already missing the girl now, how would it be like when she left him completely as soon as his wife had re-turned?

Shortly before Boltenhagen, he heard something ringing up the main road. The distant point which he saw became larger and larger, he already perceived the huffing and puffing of the excited horse.

He sprang to the side.

"Stop!" he called with a hard voice at the on-rusher.

Hedwig saw him, heard him, but she could not and did not want to bring a halt to the runaway. Only past, only not to be asked, only to be able to run riot, accompanied hard by danger.

She was already close.

"Stop!" Wilms shouted once more.

His entire head reddened. He held this swishing past to be deliberate in order to escape him. She had already flown past him at church earlier today.

"It's me, Hedwig," he roared once more.

No answer.

Ever closer.

Then the roughness, the violence rises in the farmer. He springs forward, his kind eyes threatening, a mighty blow of his fist meets the horse on its forehead so that it climbs high in the air. The sled is slung around, and the girl slams hard into the snow, where she remains lying with eyes torn wide open as if she has been struck by lightning.

"Wilms," she murmurs numbly.

He lifted her up, and still bent half over her, he gurgled, hoarse with excitement, "Hedwig, is everything okay with you? Tell me, Hedwig, is everything okay with you?"

He did not know at all what he had done.

"No, no — Wilms, I want to go home."

"Yes, we will go home, Hedwig," he burst out aghast, "come, I'll lift you into the sled." And as he lay the girl down in the vehicle which had been set right again, he felt and touched her fearfully to see whether she had any injuries.

"Hedwig, just tell me, where have you been?"

Only she sat as though paralysed.

"Don't ask me now — I want to go home."

"As you wish, then I will not ask you now," he immediately responded. "But, Hedwig, everything is okay with you, isn't it?"

She shook her head.

"Then it is just from the shock," he comforted himself and her. He took a seat next to her, grasped the reins, and the subdued brown began obediently to run at a trot.

No more words were exchanged between the pair. Hedwig sat thoughtless next to the leaseholder, and listed to the sounds of the little bells. Only once did her weak astonishment rise up over why the animal which had been so wild before now followed every movement of the driver.

She looked furtively at the man at her side, and noticed that his eyes had likewise fastened on her, full of fear.

He now looked completely different from before when he had knocked the horse back.

When she thought of it, she started as if she had herself been met by the fist.

What would come of it?

It seemed to her as if he had also subdued her with it.

VI

And the knowledge that she was slowly succumbing stirred her entire being up.

Hardly had they arrived at the farmhouse than Hedwig sat down completely exhausted in a corner of the sofa, and suddenly began sobbing violently. Wilms saw aghast that all her limbs were shaking and trembling like blades of grass over which a storm was blowing.

"Hedwig – dear Hedwig," he murmured, and he stroked her hair awkwardly. – "Are you ill? – Will you not tell me why you are crying?"

Her tears flowed more and more violently. Like a sudden rain shower which announces the storm.

"Hedwig, I cannot see what it is with you. Are you still angry with me from before?"

He meant because he had overthrown her so roughly from the sled.

"Oh, no."

She shook her head, and squeezed his hand tightly.

"Wilms – I beg you, brother-in-law," she whispered urgently. "Go out now and leave me alone – quite alone – you will do me the favour, won't you?"

"Of course, Hedwig, I'll do anything that you want," the farmer replied. "Just tell me yet, are you perhaps indignant because I went to church today without you? See, if you don't consider it proper, then I will not go anymore at all."

She just made a silent gesture in the negative, and the leaseholder stepped out heavily, bewildered. Hardly had he closed the door behind himself than Hedwig rose and threw herself completely shaken and powerless on her knees before Else's bed, where she buried her head in the pillows.

"Sister — sister," she murmured half numb with fear for her soul.

Meanwhile Wilms was striding up and down the yard in dull despair. And his bushy browed eyes turned again and again to the window behind which his ill wife had earlier lain and caused him torment. Now he peered after her healthy sister.

He grasped his forehead, and wondered.

Under him, the earth still lay firm and did not shake; above him, the snowy heavens floated and did not spit out balls of fire; around him, house and barn stood as unfaltering as usual; and yet the man who did not want to go to church anymore brooded over one of the deadly sins.

"Sins of thought," the Pastor had said once, "sins of thought."

It would get even worse.

The little farm boy approached him, and handed him a letter. It contained an invitation for that evening to go to the forester's family. The forester's wife had written it herself with a graceful script.

When Wilms entered the living room at midday, he found his young sister-in-law at the sewing table assiduously busy with a letter.

"Who are you writing to, Hedwig?" he asked timidly.

She looked up at him with a dreary smile. "To Else," she answered falteringly.

The leaseholder hesitated. “To my wife?” he repeated sombrely, and looked at the floor.

“Yes, I am asking her when she is returning.” She lowered her head at the same time, wrote a few more lines, and then handed over the sealed letter to Wilms for sending.

An oppressive silence occurred, as always happened now when the distant one was mentioned between the two.

“When she returns,” the farmer thought despondently. He straightened up. “Are you scared for her, Hedwig?”

It should have sounded indifferent, but his deep voice was gently shaking.

Trembling, the girl turned away, and did not answer.

“Just speak of something else,” Wilms thought, “of something else.” Then he mentioned the invitation which he had just received. Naturally Hedwig would decline, he thought; her pallor was conspicuous, and she had complained just before about her state of health. But to his astonishment, she cried excitedly, “Yes, we will go. Wait, I must change straightaway.”

Shaking his head, he remained behind.

Straight after coffee, they went out from the yard in the same sled which Hedwig had used that morning.

In the cosy forester’s house in the middle of the forest, things got lively. Many voices singing, violin and trumpets met them on their arrival. The forester had invited several forestry cadets from the neighbouring academy, even an assessor. The latter had brought his violin for the embellishment of the festivities. Even the Pastor’s young daughter was there.

In one of the brown-panelled rooms with the many stags’ antlers, the Christmas tree was still burning. Under it, the little blond daughter of the forester sat in her little pram and stretched her arms out to the candles.

Hedwig picked the child up and kissed it. When she turned around, Wilms stood behind her, his eyes resting on her with a strange expression.

He had thought to himself in the depths of his soul, "Why does this beautiful woman and this child not belong to me?" Slowly he brushed his hand over his forehead, and went over to the men.

It was getting late.

The evening passed into loud cheerfulness.

Hedwig was courted by the young people, Paula Schirmer nestled up to her, she had to sing. In the end, the forest assessor played dance music. Then it was natural that the girl would fly from one arm into another.

Only Wilms stood seriously to the side, he considered it unfitting to be dancing as long as his wife remained far off in the clinic.

Wrinkling his brow, it came over him as if his youth had passed in sadness. And as Hedwig danced charmingly, she steered all eyes to herself; only, sometimes her movements seemed too wild to him, something rushing then lay in them.

He shook his head.

"Stop, Miss Hedwig," the forester's wife also warned, "otherwise it will get too much."

She drew the girl away with her to her bedroom, and sprinkled some cologne on her heated face.

"How goes it with your sister?" she asked at the same time.

"I don't know," Hedwig replied absentmindedly.

The forester's wife stared at her. She noted that the excitement of her young visitor was unnatural. But she thought she had found the right track.

"Do you know that young Count Brachwitz has gotten engaged?" she inquired tensely.

"Yes, I have heard about it already," Hedwig nodded indifferently, and wanted to return to the others again.

The forester's wife did not understand what she should make of her. She held the girl firmly by the arm, and tapped her almost maternally on the cheeks. A stirring of sympathy for the beautiful, feverish creature came over her. At least she wanted to give her good advice, created out of the experiences of a mature woman. And quite honestly and genuinely, it came out, "Miss Hedwig, I always wanted to speak to you once about it. Don't stay any longer alone with your brother-in-law in his house. – Do you hear?"

"Why?" Hedwig turned around with a jerk.

She had turned deathly pale, only her brown eyes glowed and sparkled like fiery coals.

"Because," the woman continued strongly, "the tongues of vice in the area are already starting on it. I advise you well, if there is nothing in it, to go out of the way of the talk preferably."

Then Hedwig composed herself, all the blood shot to her heart, it hurt her so that she would have liked to have screamed aloud, for she felt that she had now reached the crossroads.

"Dear Anna," she said nevertheless stiffly erect, although her full lips shook in her pale face so that her opposite only understood her words with effort. "Such idle gossip is all the same to me. I will do what I consider right, and take fright from no one."

With that she tore herself away violently, and went into the large room through the middle of the joyful people straight to Wilms to ask him to dance.

The forester's wife turned red with indignation when she saw it, and she whispered excitedly to her husband.

"Hedwig," Wilms spoke sheepishly, "I would not like to. As long as Else is away – –"

She paid no attention to that. "Come, brother-in-law, – if I beg you?"

At the same time, she looked at him with her feverish eyes as ardently, as imploringly as if he could thereby save her life, as if her entire existence hung on this one dance.

Then it smashed over him as well. Wife – reputation – the fear of talk, everything went under in the one wish, to be permitted once to embrace and carry away this life defying being.

He seized her, violently, desperately, as if he wanted to crush her to his breast.

"Bravo," the forest assessor cried, as did the cadets, and they let their instruments cheer even louder. And amidst the sound of violin and trumpets, he swung her around, heavily, weightily, as if it were a matter of life and death.

He looked down at her.

Her face was twisted in pain, her breath was groaning as if she were gliding with every step over sharp knives, and yet she lay close and fully in his arms so that he completely lost his mind.

"Sweet, dear, Hedwig," he whispered.

She started, and shut her eyes.

Then the dance was also over, they separated hastily, and came together again only when they were leaving.

"Adieu then."

"Till we see each other again."

The forester and his wife promised to call soon on Wilms. "When your wife is back, Wilms," the forester suggested, "that is soon now."

"Yes, that is soon," Wilms confirmed quickly, "that is soon."

They sat again in the sled, the farmer had thrown a blanket over the girl so that almost nothing of her could be seen. Then they went through the nocturnal forest in which the sled bells echoed strangely.

"Ring–ing – ring–ing."

Hedwig's head leant gently against his shoulder. She was so leaden in all her limbs, sleep seemed to want to overwhelm her. Like in a dream, it went through her mind that she should not stay in the same house with this man any longer. But the silver bells shooed the ghost away again, "Ring–ing — ring–ing."

In the dark yard of Wilms's house, not a soul was to be seen. The night lay in this place blacker than elsewhere. The farmer carefully lifted his sister-in-law from the vehicle, and she tolerated it, although she felt how his arms were trembling. Then the night brightened. Something shuffled down from the house, old Krischan crept out to receive his master, a stall lantern threw a bright light over the yard. Then Hedwig freed herself fiercely.

Only in the dark hall before the door of the living room where she slept in Else's bed did the leaseholder reach his companion again.

It reigned black as a crow here.

Timidly he grasped her hand, and pressed it shyly.

"Hedwig," he whispered softly, and timidly touched her shoulder.

"Wilms, promise me something."

"Anything, Hedwig, that you want."

"Then send Christian out of the house, and to the old people's home."

"Yes, then he shall go," Wilms repeated without thinking. Half numbed, he bent down to her.

And the same shuffling old man whom they had just disowned rescued the pair, who did not want to be saved, for the last time.

His wooden clogs clattered on the threshold, shimmering light poured into the hall just as Hedwig, leaning against the door, felt that the floor under her was trembling and swaying, and that she would plunge into those arms which were groping for her.

"Good night, Wilms," she stuttered, starting.

"Oh, good night, Hedwig," the leaseholder lamented, and stared senselessly at the door which closed quickly behind her.

The old man had meanwhile crept past, and had found his place to sleep. Silent, weaving, impenetrable night surrounded the lonely man again.

He listened.

No sound stirred anymore, everything was asleep, only he still stood like a thief, and wanted to steal.

In there then, in there.

He knew it was unlocked.

His coarse, work-accustomed hand reached out for the handle, but it paused in the air over the brass, like at an invisible wall.

He was not capable of that. He did not dare it. The chill shook him so that his teeth chattered. He struck his hands before his face, and climbed up to his room as though wrecked and broken.

He had a bad dream.

In it he saw his wife lying on the bier, yellow and waxy. She had finally died. Violins and trumpets sounded joyfully, and he himself had Hedwig in his arms, and was dancing around the coffin jubilantly with her, and kissing her on the mouth. The corpse however lay in its wedding dress, and opened its eyes and Pastor Schirmer preached over her, "Throw the burden from yourself. Be brave."

He tossed and turned in sweat, and cried out so loudly that he awoke.

VII

Thus the winter had faded away. The snow melted. Spring storms bowed and whipped the poplars of the country road, blinding sunshine reflected in every laugh, it began to shimmer green on the birch trees, and on a fresh morning, Hedwig, standing bare-headed in the yard, perceived rustling wingbeats before her ears so that she had to look up for them.

With loud chirping, the house swallows were circling the roof and seeking their nest.

The girl, standing there completely enveloped in sunlight, placed her hand before her eyes, and looked up. Yes, it was true, spring was drawing over the land again. She had now been living almost a year in this farmstead.

And still Else had not returned.

From week to week, it was prolonged. Something always stepped between again, months came and went. If Hedwig had not thrust out her inheritance again to the leaseholder, he would have not been able to cover the fees for the past weeks. The more so as he now needed everything available for the seed-time. It often drew his forehead anxiously into creases, but Hedwig had forced the sum on him, impatiently, stormily. Then he had taken it. They belonged together, the recollection of Else became rarer now. Letters indeed arrived weekly from the invalid who reported an ever progressing improvement, but these reminders had lost their edge, and seemed to come from an indeterminate distance. Else's image gradually became impersonal to them and passed away.

Instead they had mutually joined ever closer to one another. Wilms regarded the quiet winter's days as the happiest of his life. Yes, he had a home again to which he hurried back inspired. Everything was again steady, comfortable, and ordered. He had also used the winter's leisure hours to learn from her. They had sat together under the large floor lamp, and read the modern books which Hedwig had sent to them. Even his political views were clarified by her. And gradually he began to look on near and far with different eyes. The slavish fear of God which sees a henchman in the Highest, a little spy and peeker in the pots, vanished for him, at first timidly, but soon he began more confidently to differentiate for himself good and evil according to the example of his beloved. The timid man awoke, he rose as though from a grave, and looked around at the world with astonishment. Fresh air wafted everywhere, right also belonged everywhere to the strong.

Yes, the haze of sickness had been extracted from his home.

And Hedwig loved her student. In the rich giving and sharing, she forgot that she yearned for him. Her exuberant nature found gratification.

Visitors also came to them often. Once the forester's family visited with their cadets, then Pastor Schirmer with his daughter, occasionally even the Superintendent from Boltenhagen, and quite often the pot-bellied county physician from Grimmen. Only the Pastor's wife held back. Hedwig did not ask about her, and did not seek a reason.

Then there was music and singing, frequently also dancing or serious conversation, and everyone felt stimulated by the clever, ingratiating girl. Wilms gradually became proud of her.

Her adversary, the deaf Krischan, had been removed from the farm. But that had not come about as smoothly and was now the cause of too much displeasure.

"Where shall I?" the old man had asked when Wilms revealed his decision a little hesitantly. "Where shall I go?" At the same time, he lifted his deaf ear and waggled his head impotently.

"To the old people's home. There you will be okay."

"No," the old man breathed, and chewed unsavourily with his stubbled chin, "I've been on this spot now all of fifty five years. – Your wife promised me that I could die here."

Wilms became impatient. "My wife is gone now though," he cried vehemently.

"She will come back though," the old man grinned, and laughed, chewing.

That was too much for the farmer. Hedwig had been right about it too. A date for departure was quickly and decisively set for the deaf man.

The old man listened to the decision calmly.

But when the day arrived, the old man was nowhere to be found. Servants and maids sought all over the house for him in vain, even his sleeping posy was empty, already the staff were putting it about that the old man, whom nobody could suffer, had drowned himself in the pond. Then Dörthe, the head maid, discovered a sign. She heard a croaking raven's cry above, and when she looked up, she saw how the ruffled bird of the missing man flew into the open hatch of the hayloft.

There they found him. In the deepest corner, hidden in warm hay, he lay and defended himself half mad against the servants. A policeman took him and his belongings finally from the farm, and delivered both to the old people's home. There he became ill, and people thought about his death. Only in a few days, he recovered with the good nursing, and under the charge of the doctors. And soon he was seen daily doddering along the country road up to Wilms's house where he sat on a gravestone, and stared into the farmstead.

Nobody could deny him that, the road was free. If Hedwig came over, he shook, and grinned to himself.

"He will again get the house over his head," Wilms murmured once grimly.

Hedwig talked him out of it.

At the castle in Boltenhagen in the meantime, a great feast was being celebrated. The young lord's fiance had made a call on the old Count. Hedwig saw her drive past, and the young Count who sat next to his chosen one had greeted her earnestly and deferentially. He turned around to her once more. In the evening, a magnificent set of fireworks sprayed up above. Flares and rockets hissed through the still winter air, and Wilms, leaning out the window with Hedwig, turned to her apprehensively as if he wanted to fathom her eyes. But she smiled wistfully, and looked up at him candidly. Then the anxious man was calm again.

Whoever attains riches after a long time of poverty becomes a miser, and fears losing again what has been won.

The most beautiful thing though which Hedwig had won from the bleak possession was the garden behind the house. At seed-time, when Wilms spent most of his time in his fields, she had with Dörthe taken possession of the long-neglected wilderness. Beets were dug, both native and exotic flower seeds were planted, paths were staked out, carpets of lawn set out. The giant apple tree in the middle was pruned, the rampant currant and gooseberry hedges were trimmed into orderly borders, the most difficult task though was carried out with the scattered lilac saplings. Hedwig had a thin arbour knocked up, and the saplings set all around it. The good gardner in heaven gave his blessing to it, he let warm rain on his part trickle down on pleasant nights, and when the storks appeared on the shingle roof of the house, then the branches had shot together, and the white and blue lilac bushes had formed an aromatic roof, and on bright moonlit evenings, the arrivals watched the leaseholder and his young companion sitting in the arbour, and listened as they both sang together happy and sad ballads.

Such sounds had rarely been heard there.

The lilac scattered its flowers over them, and from the blossoming apple tree, a wonderful scent streamed across, the father stork flapped gently in dreaming in between. But for both the children below, the heart beat ardently and fully, and they still remained silent.

***

It was an evening in May. Wilms, Hedwig and little Pastor Schirmer were sitting in the lilac arbour, and chatting about this and that. A hurricane lamp glowed on the table. The breeze was so light that even the tiny clergyman sat bareheaded with his sparse silver locks.

Then a heavy step crunched along the path. A few branches were pushed aside, and the massive figure of the forester became visible.

"Good evening my friends," he called jovially, and shook the hand of everyone. "You have a beautiful little spot here – truly. – Evening, Miss Hedwig, I brought something quite special with me for you –" he chirruped with his tongue – "here."

With that, he offered the girl a heavy bundle of green herbs. They exhaled a spicy aroma.

"Woodruff?" Hedwig said surprised.

"Correct – my wife picked them herself. It flowers so splendidly that – –"

"That you must not let it go to waste," the young hostess completed charmingly, "how would it be, master forester, if we brewed a bowl up straightaway? You have nothing against it?"

"Against it?" the huntsman cried, and looked around as triumphantly as if he had just managed a good work. "That's why I tucked them to myself straightaway. And with you in the kitchen, Miss Hedwig? — Well, if my wife knew that I now give in to cooking. But that shall be a sip, please be careful, Pastor, of what comes of it."

The others gave applause. And after a short time, Hedwig appeared again with a large tureen, the forester behind her carrying a bottle of hock under his arm. "If it's too thin," he explained with twinkling eyes.

But it was not too thin.

They clinked glasses, the hurricane lamp reflected reddishly in the yellow liquid, the silver tones rang out into the May night.

"Beautiful," the forester cried, and laid his hands contentedly on his torso, "very beautiful."

"Thank you, Hedwig," Wilms said with a long admiring look, and raised his glass.

And the little Pastor licked his lips, and nodded, smiling thoughtfully, "The Bible has a toast for it, my friend," he said to himself, and folded his hands around the glass. "Psalm 65 — 11, 12 and 13*."

"Yes," the forester said approvingly, "very beautiful." He was already holding his third cup, and nobody knew whether he was admiring so much the fitting verse or Hedwig's successful bowls. Then he drew forth a little packet from the Stralsund factory, and spoke half beseeching, half bashful, "A game of skat?"

And without waiting, he continued, "Wilms deals."

Smiling the gentlemen grasped the cards, the cigars were lit, and soon the accustomed words fell, "Tournée? — Solo? — Pastor, don't show me your cards."

---

* [11]Thou crownest the year with thy goodness; and thy paths drop fatness. [12]They drop the pastures of the wilderness: and the little hills rejoice on every side. [13]The pastures are clothed with flocks; the valleys also are covered over with corn; they shout for joy, they also sing.

Hedwig left the arbour quietly. She slowly walked about in the garden, the moon stood full in the sky and illuminated the narrow paths. At a blossoming pink hawthorn, the girl turned, and looked back at the bright arbour. There the three sat under the white and blue lilac bushes, sipped the good wine, and played on animatedly.

It had an effect like a picture of cosiness.

"And that you created," it wanted to call up in Hedwig, but she did not express it, just a feeling of ease and pride came over her.

She opened the garden gate inaudibly, walked quietly across the silent yard until she had reached the entrance to the country road.

Here she had first arrived a year ago. Much had changed since then.

Resting, she looked down the country road. There everything breathed a deep stillness, blue-grey twilight stretched between the trunks of the poplars, only the crickets were chirpings in the ditches without interruption.

Then a distant rolling sounded in between. It became quiet again, but then – from a turn in the main road, you could hear the distinct sound of whips and the approach of a carriage. A pair of lanterns sparkled.

Hedwig stepped back. Did the vehicle not come from Boltenhagen? Where would a coach be going so late? Could someone in the Count's family have become ill?

The chaise stopped directly before the entrance to the farmstead where the girl was standing.

Hedwig's heart began pounding.

From the leather carriage, an ungainly head stretched itself out, and a reserved voice called, "Miss Schröder? Are you Miss Schröder? I'm Rosenblüt from Grimmen, you know, a good friend of your father."

Hedwig stepped up to the coach, and offered the businessman her hand. Taken aback, she asked whether he had a message for her from the town.

The merchant rocked his head, “Don’t you know yet? That is, how would you know?” he repeated to himself. “I met the county doctor there today, Rumpf – also treated me for my gallstone, made bad jokes all the time, constantly said, ‘You must stop, Mr Rosenblüt, you are already a rock of the town.’”

“Yes, but Mr Rosenblüt – –”

The merchant pondered, “Then the county doctor instructed me to make a surprise visit on you. Now, you still don’t know? Your sister is back – with your father – and tomorrow she will arrive here.”

“Who is back?” Hedwig asked quite softly.

“Well, Mrs Wilms. And she’ll look, I tell you, as healthy as you and I. Can only imagine. It will be a great joy for you. Well, give my regards to Mr Wilms – I’ll let you congratulate him. – Good night, Miss Schröder.”

“Thank you most kindly,” Hedwig said, and offered him her hand.

The carriage rolled away.

“A strangely calm girl,” the merchant thought as he pressed himself back into his cushions. “She remains always the same – in joy and sorrow.”

Hedwig walked slowly back across the yard, and entered the garden again. For a long time, she stood behind the illuminated arbour, and plucked thoughtlessly at a branch of white lilac. Within the gentlemen had shoved their cards together, there were clinking glasses once more in farewell, and the forester stretched, gathered his winnings, and hummed to himself:

In forest and on heath,
There I seek my delight,
I am a hunting man,
I am a hunting man.

The ballad rang jovially out into the night. And the little Pastor, who could not tolerate much drink, shoved his arm under that of the singer, and murmured indistinctly, “Dear friend – you – you will accompany me home, won’t you?”

“Of course – will be done, Pastor,” the forester laughed with a sideways glance, “everyone will be delivered on time. Good night, Wilms, my regards to little Hedwig. A splendid thing. Thunderbolts, if I were young – if I were young –”

“Good night.”

The two gentlemen went off, Wilms accompanied them to the entrance, and even on the main road, you could hear the forester singing the hunting song.

Wilms returned to the garden cheerfully. When he entered the arbour, he found Hedwig there, sitting at the table, and with her head propped in her hand.

He faltered.

“Hedwig, dear? – I thought you had already gone to bed?”

“No, Wilms, I wanted to wait for you still.”

“Really? – That’s nice. – Well, then come, Hedwig, we’ll drink a last glass together. – We haven’t clinked glasses together today yet. – Will you?”

He sat down opposite her, and pushed a full glass before her, but she acted so unmoving, she had dropped her head so bleakly, that Wilms stared at her strangely.

“Hedwig, are you perhaps ill?” he stuttered.

“No, no, brother-in-law –” she straightened up, and smiled a little. “I even have something very good to share with you.”

“Very good? – And yet you look so sad?”

“Sad?” she replied in bewilderment, and suddenly a deep pallor covered her face. Wilms saw how her hands moved trembling. “The spring air probably – I have a headache – I am so pleased for you – Wilms, Else has returned to Grimmen, and arrives here tomorrow."

The farmer let his glass sink down, and took a deep breath.

Then she told him everything. "And," she concluded uncertainly, "she shall have been made whole. – Thank God." But she avoided looking at him.

Wilms stirred, "Thank God," he murmured mechanically. Then he stretched, laid his hand on his forehead, and stepped wordlessly into the garden. His figure stooped at the same time as if he were carrying something.

After some time, he slowly returned. His face twitched as he took his place again opposite her. The kindhearted blue eyes seemed quite shadowed by his bushy eyebrows. He stretched his hand out, and grasped hers.

"Thank you for everything, Hedwig, everything that you have done for me," he spoke with trembling voice, and clasped her fingers spasmodically, "also, Hedwig, for bringing a little contentment again into my house. – I have felt so well –" he murmured softly, and a large, heavy drop emerged from his eye, "God ordains it so everything remains so."

Then Hedwig lowered her head down onto his hand, and remained lying unmoving so that he saw her golden brown plaits shimmering in the fleeting glow of the hurricane lamp. Her forehead burned on his skin.

The man's chest rose ever more arduously. Gently he drew his hand back.

"We don't want to make it any harder for ourselves, Hedwig," he said, mobilising all his powers. "It is not easy. – Come, Hedwig, shall we toast to always remaining good friends like today."

Slowly she rose. Slender and erect, she stood before him as she grasped the glass, but her eyes hung on his, so insistently, so unavoidably, so violently serious that he was almost frightened by them.

The Bible has words for this love, “Vehement as the flame of the Lord and strong as death.”*

The glasses clinked together, they looked each other once more in the eyes, then they offered each other their hands, and walked back silently to the farmstead.

VIII

“Welcome” stood written over the front door, and green girlands with red and white garden flowers decorated the posts when the mistress of the house stepped for the first time again over the threshold.

Wilms and Hedwig had jointly fetched her from the train station.

“Oh, how beautiful you have made everything for me,” Else whispered excitedly as she entered the hall hand in hand with her husband, and threw herself on his chest.

“Oh God, how I thank you that you let me live to see it. – Is the Pastor not awaiting me here?” she added eagerly.

“No, my child,” Wilms responded, “I thought it would be just us at first.”

Else nodded, “Yes, you are right. Come quick into the room.” And when they had entered the large living

* Cf. Song of Solomon 8:6.

room, where a festive table decorated with flowers awaited her, she embraced her sister, and kissed her stormily on the mouth, “Dear Hedwig, that is from you. No, how pleased I am that I am again in my own home. And completely recovered again as well.” – She placed herself before the mirror, and took off her hat. “Don’t you think, Wilms,” she continued hastily, “none of it is noticeable at all anymore? I look almost again like at our wedding? – Or do you think not?”

“Yes, my child,” Wilms answered bleakly, “you are much – much recovered.”

He and Hedwig threw a look at each other at the same time. Both noticed how hectically red her cheeks were coloured, and what deep blue rings rimmed the eyes of the homecomer. Her figure was gently stooped forward, and even her shoulders were drawn forward. And yet the narrow face still allowed traces of earlier beauty to be recognised.

In the meantime, Else had again turned to her husband, she laid both hands on his chest, and cried between laughing and crying, “Are you not pleased then, Wilms, that I am here again? You are so quiet.”

Tenderly she lifted her mouth up to him, and shut her eyes as Wilms bent down to her gravely and without a word. But as he did that, his look skimmed the younger woman anxiously. Hedwig had silently turned to the window.

“And now we will go to the table,” cried Else. “You shall see how much I can eat now. No more like before.”

With these words, she settled down on the sofa, which Hedwig had already placed by the table, and drew Wilms next to her.

The sister had sit down opposite them on a chair.

Then she dispensed the dishes herself in eager animation, yes, the homecomer seemed to want to recover again in one day all that she had missed in her domestic duties during the long years of her illness. At a minimum she wanted to show her freshly won strength to her husband so that he would delight in it.

And then she began to tell of her experiences in the clinic.

Wilms brow darkened more and more.

For many moons, not the slightest indication during his intercourse with Hedwig had reminded him anymore that his home had once been like an infirmary in which only negotiations about doctors, illness, and medicines had been carried out. Now, as Else intricately described the sufferings she had survived, that tepid smell of illness and decay which had oppressed his senses for years seemingly rose again.

Seeking help, he looked to Hedwig, but the girl seemed to be listening attentively, and not sharing in his aversion. That ruined the first lunch for him completely. He only still held the knife and fork in his hands for appearances, yes, he thanked God when his wife, who despite her reputed appetite had only nipped fleetingly from everything, finally rose from the table.

"Do you know, Hedwig," she said to her sister, and tapped her cheeks maternally as she stood up, "You are looking pale. You have surely overstrained yourself here in recent times. But now everything shall be different. Oh, Wilms, how happy I am that I will now be able to take everything in hand myself. And watch out for how quickly I find my feet again. Then I will also take neat care of you, my dear Hedwig."

The woman being addressed smiled wistfully, and again her and the farmer's eyes met in a long meaningful look.

It was already the third time that they had spoken so silently and sadly to each other.

Depressed and incapable of controlling himself any longer, Wilms finally broke free. He took leave of his wife to go out into the fields to check on the sowing.

But the old game repeated itself, Else quickly snatched at his hand.

"Wilms, you don't want to leave me alone already now?" she cried with a soft tone of displeasure, "straightaway on the first day I am here?"

At the same time, her cheeks turned a glowing red, and she gnawed with her teeth at her lower lip, "You won't do that, will you?"

Here it was already evident that the half-recovered woman would not be able to bear an upset or an argument at all.

The farmer remained standing.

So that was his future? Should he again be shackled so that he was bound and handed over unopposed to the ensuing hardship again?

The fear for his existence which had already filled him once, and which had been just recently exorcised by that still, silent girl there, the paralysing horror wanted to seize him anew. But only for a moment, then the large man straightened up decisively, ready finally to maintain his manly dignity before the illness.

But he would not say any improvident word. Hedwig had read the vigorous movement in his countenance, and hurried quickly to help him.

"Else," she declared with her affectionate but yet so proud determination, as if an objection had been barred from the outset, and laid her hand gently on her arm, "Your husband has no more time for us, you must let him go. Too much loss of money is at play if he is delayed during these months."

The ill woman threw a surprised look at her sister, "So?" she then spoke, still a little sharply, "you seem to have learnt much here about farming already, Hedwig?"

Only quite unexpectedly, she gave in, and waved smiling with her hand that he should go.

"Just go, Wilms — go. You are right. It is true. It just seems to me as if I could not at all part from you now — but just go."

Then Wilms went out ponderously and depressed. And as he slowly strode across his fields, which were being raked and sown, then he felt in a sore mood, much worse than when his wife had lain in her sickbed. How would it end?

In the midst of his hard work, everything danced about him in confusion. Hedwig's questioning eyes, her glorious figure, her red lips, and next to them again the delicate, nervous image of the homecomer huddling tenderly close to him to kiss him.

He shuddered, all around hot summer haze lay on the earth, and yet it seemed to him as if something cold had just touched his mouth. A vehement, physical repugnance crept over him when he recalled his wife's caresses.

"No — no — God save me — preserve me from that. — I must not think of it — Karl, Jochen," he called out loudly to his people.

He wanted to have men around him to shoo the spectres into the midst of the sunlight.

***

Meanwhile both sisters were alone.

Hedwig advised the ill woman that she should lie down now for a bit, only Else did not want to know about it, although her movements since Wilms's leaving had become visibly weaker.

"No, no, Hedwig," she hastily refused, "believe me, I don't need that now anymore. We will now instead look over the household a bit, above all things my cupboards.

I have looked forward to it for weeks. Have you kept them neatly in order?"

The other woman confirmed sufferingly, and opened a clothes cupboard in the living room, but for Else it all went too slowly. In her haste, she tore the bunch of keys from the younger woman's hand, and ran with it from one cupboard to another. She looked everywhere. Then she hung the keys on her belt.

"I would prefer now to keep them to myself again," she declared to Hedwig with a face reddening with delight. "From now on, I will oversee everything again." And she kissed her sister stormily on the cheek, "You are pleased about it, Hedwig, aren't you?"

The younger woman nodded earnestly. A wistful smile played around her lips when the clinking things adorned her sister's belt again.

Now she had been thus deposed, she was superfluous. Despondently she looked at the floor. There was no struggle against it. Her staying in the room became oppressive for her.

"Come, Else," she pulled herself together, "I have a surprise for you. Come with me."

She intended to show the homecomer the place which had been previously covered in wild scrub, and had been transformed now under Hedwig's hand into a blossoming garden.

They strode hither.

And Else's rapture was at first quite proper. Silent and blissful, she slung her arm around Hedwig's shoulders, and both sisters sat thus in the blossoming lilac arbour, and dreamed away in the sinking, rosy day.

Hedwig recalled to herself the previous evening. In her ears, the silver tones rang again, like the day before, when her glass had touched with that of the farmer.

From now on, Else would sit thus with her husband here, the girl thought, but she would go. She let her hands fall into her lap, and looked over the gooseberry hedges away to the adjoining wide green meadow on which countless butterflies were flitting about in the last of the evening sunlight.

"You are so quiet?" Else asked.

In the same moment, Wilms returned. He was pleased to find both women at the increasingly loved place, and told Else how often they had eaten there cosily. He concluded by asking her to keep to this custom today as well.

Else looked astonished at the man standing before her.

"Here?" she asked taken aback. "But here won't it soon be too cool?"

"God forbid, Else," Wilms refuted, "we sat here just yesterday with Hedwig, even late into the night."

"So?" Else responded, stretching the word out. A light cloud drew over her brow, the folds around her mouth were stamped somewhat sharper, it was only a quite light intimation of rancour, and vanished again just as quickly as it had arisen.

Yet no suspicion been had awoken in the suffering woman.

"Then you have enjoyed yourselves quite well in my absence," she suggested, shrugging her shoulders.

She smiled at the same time as if she held it all to be a jest, and caressed her sister's hand. Straightaway, however, she writhed her shoulders.

Just then the sun had vanished behind red smouldering strips, a tepid little breeze skimmed over the meadow.

"I am getting too cold," Else said faintly, and rose quickly, "and I think we will therefore prefer to eat in the living room. We are in favour of being all three together again."

Immediately the others also rose. The will of the ill woman was mightier than there own inclinations. Custom and habit always offered the same considerate subordination.

Thoughtfully Hedwig laid a shawl across her shoulders, Else took the arm of the younger woman, and after all the self-imposed stress of this day, she strolled weakly and wearily next to her youthfully fresh guide.

Wilms followed them.

He looked darkly at the two so different figures, but he did not dare to compare them anymore. Only at the exit of the garden, he turned back once more to the blossoming lilac arbour. A heady scent wafted over.

"Even that gone," Wilms murmured. In a fluster, he broke away. The life's joy fled from him like a bird whistling past, and the dreary spirit of despair cast a shadow again with its dark bat's wings.

IX

The next morning, the fat county physician appeared. From his outward behaviour, you could decipher with difficulty what he thought of the state of the leaseholder's wife. He indeed kissed her fingertips a few times, but with restraint.

That was a strange sign, for patients in whom the beloved old Dr Rumpf delighted, he graced with his stormy tenderness.

But with Else, he behaved almost with pity. He brushed the fine blond hair from her forehead after the examination, and said affectionately, as though to a child, "Well, it's working. But conserving, my child always nicely conserving. Just proper quiet, that is the main thing."

With that he took himself into the garden where Wilms and Hedwig were already waiting for him.

"Yes," he suggested with a shake of the head, "it has come to a stop with your wife, dear Wilms – we want to hope for the best. But no excitement, you hear, you must pay attention to that, I tell you expressly, an excitement would be pure poison for the ill woman."

When the physician had left the farm shortly afterward, the leaseholder and the girl remained for a moment standing next to each other in the garden.

Deep dejection was painted in the honest features of the farmer.

"Hedwig," he finally began hoarsely, while he looked around timidly, and his chest heaved as violently as if he were sighing under the weight of a mountain, "It is terrible what constantly goes around in my head, but is it true you will not have any loathing of me? Hedwig," he grasped her hand, and wheezing, he whispered further, as if it were a secret, "I cannot bear the uncertainty anymore, it's beyond my powers. I wish it were in any case, bend or break, either she were healthy, or – she went from us."

With that he stared up with raised head despairingly into the blue sky as if he expected a consoling answer from there above.

But nothing stirred, only the wind leading meadow scents into the garden.

Wilms suddenly squeezed his head with both hands, and groaned aloud, "Good God – how can I even think such a thing? — — I have surely already gone crazy myself — already crazy," he repeated mutely.

"Why shouldn't you entertain a wish?" Hedwig spoke forlornly to herself.

She had until now stood like a white marble statue opposite the sorrow of the man she wanted to make happy, but while she spoke those last words, her large eyes opened wide with fright. Motionless, she stared into the distance. Something red and bloody was flickering vaguely towards her there, her heart pounded to bursting, and when she looked once more at Wilms, she turned deathly pale.

Horror.

She must have seen something gruesome.

Without farewell, the two parted from each other. Soon afterwards, Wilms entered the living room to say goodbye to his wife. He found Else sitting heartily and assiduously at her sewing table, eagerly occupied with stitching together some linen thing.

"Where is Hedwig?" she asked quickly at his entrance, and lifted her bright eyes.

Wilms hesitated, "Probably in the kitchen," he responded awkwardly. He lied. Something unexpected, and dark forced him to.

His wife slowly let her work sink into her lap, and looked at him. Dörthe, the head maid, had just told her that Hedwig had stepped into the garden with her master. And yet he said that he had not met up with her sister?

She breathed quickly, her fingers trembled a little, in her haste she pricked herself with the needle so that a little drop of blood welled up.

Wilms wanted quickly to bind it up with a handkerchief. She fended him off, "Leave it. — It's nothing," she said firmly, although her voice gently trembled. Then she turned, and looked out the window quietly for a while. When she again turned her countenance to her husband, it had won back its old expression, only her eyes watched thoughtfully and brooding to herself.

"Adieu, Wilms," she said somewhat forced, and after she had reached out her hands, she asked her husband, "Send Christian in to me at once. He shall carry an invitation to the Pastor."

Wilms was already standing at the door. He became embarrassed. "Who should I — — ?" he asked hesitantly.

"Old Christian now."

"Oh, he — — yes — he — Else — I dismissed him."

Wilms knew that he had incurred an injustice, he had chased out the old man out of love for the beautiful woman before whose room he had stood at the time. The man had served on the farm for a lifetime. The sweat broke out on his forehead, in his self-consciousness he was scraping back and forth with his boots on the sand strewn stone floor of the room, and dared not raise his eyes to his wife. But Else sat quite silently at first. "You dismissed old Christian?" she murmured finally disbelieving. "Seriously?"

The leaseholder nodded.

The ill woman flared up, "But don't you know that I had promised the old man he could close out his life here!" she cried outraged.

In vehement displeasure, she threw her linen down, and pressed both hands to her temples. Her eyes, the rims of which were darkening more and more, began to shine morbidly.

Wilms also noticed it. Full of fear, he stepped closer, "You should not get excited, Else," he begged breathlessly. "Do you hear, my child, not because of that."

Only, Else's patience had been exhausted. A stream of tears burst forth, she tossed the scissors onto the floor so that they rattled, and was quite distraught.

"I want to know finally what has been going on here behind my back?" she cried outraged, although she was struggling for air. "Why did you send the old man away, why?"

"Because he had behaved outrageously."

"Towards you?"

Then the question came. Wilms stuttered. The blood climbed in his head.

"Towards me – Else? – No, not that exactly."

"Towards whom then?"

"Towards – towards your sister – towards Hedwig."

Else started painfully. Then she rose quickly, and made a few contradictory movements.

"And then Hedwig surely asked too," she sobbed furiously, "that he should go? – Isn't that right?"

But the outbreak of her fury itself made the farmer stubborn. Over his nose, a few deep folds constricted, "Of course," he responded slowly, "I did it at Hedwig's request."

Then the suffering woman lost all hold.

"But she had no business in asking here," she screamed now quite senselessly. "What concern is it of my sister, when you know quite well that I never, ever would give my agreement to this dismissal? – Just tell me what concern is it of Hedwig's?"

She wanted to complain even more, but suddenly she broke off, and her look directed itself bewilderedly at her husband.

What was happening so fast to him?

He looked at her entirely, the awkward giant, as if he were seeing this weak female for the first time. His fists balled themselves and opened again, his chest moved heavily, strangely.

"Else," it came out dully, as he approached her ponderously – "now that is enough – now I want to hear nothing more of it, you are ill, that I grant in your favour."

He spoke gravely and insistently like he had never spoken before. It sounded hard and dry, as if stones were being thrown onto each other.

Nodding his head, he then strode to the door. But before he had reached it, his wife suddenly staggered to him to embrace his chest with her weak arms, "Wilms, I don't know what I am saying," she stammered half powerlessly, and in her pale face, her eyes closed wearily, "I – I – oh God, I will do anything out of love for you. – Do you not believe me?"

She lay powerless in his arms, Wilms had to lift her up.

"Yes, yes, that I believe," he murmured, transformed and overwhelmed by the one word – "you poor woman – come, Else."

He carried her to the sofa, and put her gently to bed.

As he bent down over her, though, she threw her arms around his neck, and lifted her lips stormily to his.

"You are okay again, aren't you?" she smiled.

"Yes, yes, Else."

An ardent kiss burned on his mouth.

Then he found himself outside, and strode, bowed as ever before, to his fields.

In a furrow lay a butterfly which had been hit by a clump of sand. Unpitying, the farmer stamped it with heavy boots into the ground.

"Good for you," he spoke roughly.

***

And the same Hedwig of whom the ill woman was beginning to become jealous entered through the doors, and brought the completely exhausted prone woman a mug of bouillon. It stirred the suffering woman, and brought her round. Though tears were still flowing from her eyes, she nevertheless drew the beautiful blossoming girl down to her, and tenderly stroked her brown, golden shimmering hair. “Hedwig, is it true,” she whispered barely audibly, “you aren’t being bad to me, are you?” And she lifted her face up to her sister, and inquired into her dark, expressive eyes, “No, no, you won’t do me harm,” she added, comforted.

Later, when Hedwig had already left again, the suffering woman, who thought herself recovered, took her Bible, and attempted to master her angry thoughts through the Holy Scripture. But she flew over the broad lines blindly, and her lips murmured all sorts of broken sounds which did not belong there. She finally rose distractedly, and strode several times uncertainly around the wide room.

“Why did he lie to me?” she pondered without being able to find an answer. Weary and tense, she finally leant out the window, and looked into the yard, over which warm sunshine lay.

Then she became attentive. What was the figure sitting there outside on the kerbstone before the gate? A doddering expired human figure crouched there, and directed his extinguished eyes rigidly at the farmstead.

The peering woman leant forward. Was that old Krischan? A strange joy befell the suffering woman. She did not ask herself whether it was fitting to traffic with the dismissed servant; hastily, with a feverish rush, she ran to him, and touched his shoulder.

The old man arduously lifted his nodding head, and when he recognised the woman in the simple, grey dress, a weak smile ran over his withered lips.

For Else, he had constantly been a faithful watchdog.

“Poor woman,” he said, and stroked her arm with his frail, trembling hand. “Poor woman.”

That was the greeting.

"No, no," Else cried loudly so that he would understand her. "I am not ill anymore, Krischan, I feel much healthier."

"Poor woman," the old man nodded unchanged, almost pitying.

Else was frightened. What did the deaf man mean by that? Without thinking, abruptly blushing, she asked him why he had offended her sister.

"Me?" the old man whispered, and raised his chin. Then he pulled himself together, and wheezed something into the waiting woman's ear.

Just a few words, but Else stumbled backward, and turned white as snow. Just a pair of bright, red stains glowed on her cheeks.

"You lie, Krischan," she screamed. "It isn't true."

Only the old man did not understand the unhappy woman, or did not let it disturb him. For he stroked her arm anew with his bony hand, and burst out with effort, "Poor woman – no, no, I saw it myself, as they sat together in the sled. The two are waiting now all impatiently."

"Waiting?" the poor woman now groaned weakly. Everything turned before her eyes. She had to lean on the wall by the entrance.

"It is for you, my poor woman, to die. They are waiting for the death of the woman. Then they will be freed."

A heart-rending scream, shrill, screeching, pierced over the country road, and was thrown back by the walls of the leaseholder's house.

The tormented woman thought she was being choked, an iron hand was grasping for her throat, the cripple's face danced around her like a hundred grimaces. Yet she gurgled something.

"Help – – help."

Then a dull fall.

"Poor woman," the old servant groaned, and bent down over her, "poor child, they have killed you, you poor girl."

***

But Else had not died.

"Didn't that sound like a cry for help?" Hedwig asked the head maid with whom she was with in the dairy. Dörthe had also heard the shrill cry. When she investigated, she found the lady of the house among the weeds by the edge of the ditch, white like a smashed statue which, in dirt and rubbish, has falled victim to oblivion.

A shattered human figure.

In falling, she had grazed a stone; a bloody scar ran from it across her forehead.

Then the beautiful girl threw herself on her knees. Her mouth opened, "Is – she dead – Dörthe?"

The maid cried out. "No, no, Miss, she is moving – lift her head up."

"Yes, yes – she's alive," Hedwig repeated, rousing her.

Thank God what had just then swished and roared before her ears was not true. – She had surely wished her death, but that had happened in a feverish dream, in a vision. – She was alive, yes – she was alive – thank God. Now it had only been thoughts, bad thoughts, but powerless – great God – she was alive, yes.

With strong arms, she embraced the rigid, twitching body, and carried it, swaying and trembling under the burden, and alone, to the maid's astonishment, without help into the large room. There she undressed her sister, and put her into the bed which again absorbed the lady of the house in its white pillows.

Yes, the ill woman returned to the linen grave.

Would it be forever?

"No, then there is still the damp, the black resting place on which the flowers bloom," Hedwig thought, sitting as before by the bed, and listening to the stirring breaths of the ill woman. And she had wished this dwelling on her sister, she brooded further, so as to solely possess her husband, whose heart already belonged to her, whom she had educated, formed, ennobled, and who yearned for her as though for salvation. The rotten body there should be lying in the grave, and the young blossoming body with the beloved husband. She started, and looked at the ill woman. In the meantime, she had won back her entire strength and deliberateness. Did not the waxen, pale face of the suffering woman look already like that of a corpse? – Yes, it was now completely clear to Hedwig. The ill woman below – she herself above. It was the right thing, not a sin, to wish it, just the course of nature.

She rose quietly to go look out the window at the country road, and see whether Wilms and the doctor she had immediately sent for would have arrived yet. At the same time, she had to pass the tall mahogany framed mirror. Instinctively she stopped before it, and set her bodice right.

The glass showed a beautiful woman aspiring to maturity, quite born to acting, creating, and making happy. She smiled melancholically when she examined herself. She was still looking into it when something appeared strange to her. The bed behind her was also reflected in the pane, and now – was she mistaken? No, the pillows were moving, the gaunt figure was straightening up, and a pair of darkly shrouded eyes were staring at her.

"Hed – wig," something groaned.

She flew to Else and grasped her hand, the ill woman looked at her glassily as if she were trying to think.

"How did I get here?" she whispered, and fingered the pillows of the bed anxiously.

Suddenly she thrust herself towards Hedwig's breast, but suddenly pushed her sister away with the most vehement abhorrence.

"Else, it's me," Hedwig cried alienated, "don't you recognise me?"

Only the pitiable woman seemed to be already raving. She rolled around groaning, and covered her eyes with a pillow as if she wanted to flee the sight of her sister.

"Yes, I recognise you," she whimpered with such a shrill voice that it penetrated through the younger woman like a sharp needles. "You wormed your way in here to steal my happiness from me. — You are only waiting for my death! — — But I won't die yet — I will not make place for you — I will live — you hear, I will live!"

Hedwig understood what it was about. It ran coldly down her spine. Her look always directed at the sobbing woman rumpled in pain, she groped backwards to the table, and clasped its edge firmly. She had to hold onto herself too. Everything was swaying and falling in her, but during the daze, she still clenched her teeth defiantly.

Never was she as beautiful as in this silent struggle with the dying woman.

Then the feverish woman pulled herself together again, and clawed with both her fists at her sister. The most extreme paroxysm had been reached. Hedwig was horrified. The decayed woman looked wraithlike with the black shadow in her face already, as if a dead woman were still shaking her fists.

"Get out of my sight," the poor woman shrieked — "away — away — I don't want to see you — you want to poison me — ! — You have seduced my husband too, — you were with him tonight — I know everything — Jesus

Christ, you adulterer! – Jesus – for pity." Then a long rattle, and she fell back powerless on her bed.

In the same moment, Wilms entered the room.

X

A gentle May day was coming to an end. On the horizon, magnificent colours were dissolving. A play of yellow, deep blue, and red rippled through each other, and the last reddish light was falling through the branches of the lilac arbour. A gentle breeze wafted through the garden, otherwise everything breathed reassurance and evening stillness.

But this peaceful environment was marred by the wild commotion which had broken out in the leaseholder's house.

Servants and maids crept around as timidly and soundlessly as before, the door hinges were greased so that the ill woman would not be disturbed by creaking, everything in the house was veiled again in silence, a dull, sombre solemnity pressed down again on the people and the farmstead.

In the evening, the county physician had arrived, and remained now alone in the large living room. It became quieter and quieter in the house, only occasionally a shrill cry of pain could be heard from the ill woman's room.

In the lilac arbour, however, sat two silent people who started when such a wailing sound arose, and held their breath to hear if it would recur.

It was becoming more and more hidden and dusky around them; behind tree and bush, bright, white mist was swelling up, and the two scared people could barely still recognise their features.

"Hedwig, now go to my wife," the leaseholder finally requested inarticulately, while he shifted still deeper into the shadows of the arbour, "and find out why the doctor hasn't returned at all."

With that the tall figure collapsed into itself again, and brooded so lost in itself that the farmer did not notice how Hedwig did not follow out his wish, but remained quietly sitting next to him.

Finally she brushed the hair from her forehead. That alerted Wilms.

"Hedwig, don't you want to — — ?"

"No, brother-in-law, I won't go to your wife."

"You — won't go?"

"No — no — please, Wilms — let me not go in anymore."

"Yes — but — Hedwig, why?"

"Because — because I am frightened by her," it came shaking over her lips.

The leaseholder stared at her — blindly — and seized hold of his head.

Yet the leaseholder did not know what had played out that morning between the two sisters. Hedwig had silently locked everything away in herself; the sensitive, soft hearted man did not need to learn that they had been discovered, that their secret desire which had never been uttered, which was still wish without fulfillment, that this was already watched for and cursed by the departing woman who now would soon not disturb them anymore.

She wanted coldly and proudly to keep everything away from him so as to remain herself in wait until salvation was finally there — the beginning of happiness.

But now – now, when the wild sounds of pain penetrated out into the quiet garden, now she could not bear it. Then she was seized by horror, and trembled. It lay like ice around her heart. Was she really guilty that a human life had to depart in there? Had she really driven a despairing woman to her death?

A cry of pain struck her ears again.

It overwhelmed her, she was no match for it, everything in her screamed for solace – peace – forgiveness.

A word of love would spare her, a single word from the man to whom she wanted to give her youth, to whom she wanted to dedicate herself, unconditionally, now, when it would also be forever, because he had infatuated her with his stupid helplessness from the outset.

But the leaseholder sat there worried, and did not stir.

Then Hedwig let her hands sink into her lap, and murmured despairingly, "I wish I were the one who could lie in eternal peace, and everything would remain the same at your place until you're old. – I would so like to die."

But death had no power over her yet, on the contrary, life struck blustering over her.

Wilms seized her hand spasmodically, "What – Hedwig?" he stammered, "No, no – just not you – that I could not bear – just not you – we will remain together." He embraced her, and pressed her to himself.

And then it was suddenly there, what had for many moons crept nearer and nearer.

Without hesitation, she felt his trembling lips on her own, she flung her arms around the man's powerful neck and, amidst aching kisses, she noticed how his tears moistened her face. She too was sobbing. As if they wanted to console each other, they lay in each others arms.

It was not a joyful discovery.

***

In the wide, uncomfortable living room, it had meanwhile become quieter. The fat county physician had concluded his examination and asked the heavily suffering woman sparingly what had so suddenly thrown her into agitation. For a long time, the weak woman had withstood his pressing, but finally, when the old gentleman took her so paternally and kindly in his arms, she took heart and, like a small child nestled against the old friend, she whispered to him falteringly and crying her terrible discovery.

"Oh God, that I would not have believed – but it is true, doctor, Krischan himself saw it."

The old doctor shook his head, and argued with complete conviction against such ideas. "Oh, nonsense – my child – servants' gossip."

"Really?" she breathed weakly. A beam of hope broke from her eyes.

"Of course – I know both of them too well."

"Oh, yes," the prone woman whispered thankfully, then she raised her weary eyes to the ceiling, on which the burning lamp was throwing its yellow circle, and squeezed the physician's hand in closing, "I don't believe it either," she said with trembling lips, "no, I don't believe it – don't believe it."

Wilms entered.

His wife smiled at him, and moved her lips. But what she wanted was indecipherable.

The doctor bent over her.

"Wilms, your wife wishes to see her sister too," he explained then, and took himself into the garden to fetch the girl. He found her in the arbour. Darkness already reigned.

"Does Else want me?" Hedwig spoke confusedly, but did not allow the friend of many years to notice the unease which stormed in her.

"Yes, we will go to her."

What a walk. The first kisses still burned on her mouth, yet she did not know how it was all possible, and what would now ensue.

"Will she suffer for long?" she inquired breathlessly.

Had the little physician heard the trembling wish in this question? Before the door to the house, he stopped, and stroked her wavy hair thoughtfully.

"Yes, she can still suffer for a long time," he responded in a low voice, "and hence – Hedwig, I think it would be good if you now left here permanently."

"Me?" She was frightened; – did he know something already?

The stay here has not done you well. You arrived here as a lady, and – I don't know, but you have out here taken on something hard, rustic, and – it would really be good for everyone, you understand," he broke off, "if you went back to your father."

No answer.

Rigid and wide-eyed, the girl looked through the darkness at the old friend. She was in a mood now to fall on his neck to confess and confide to him all the tormenting thoughts which flickered greedily around the death of her own sister. But her strength was not yet exhausted.

She composed herself, and calmly gave the doctor her answer, "Above all things, my duty is to stay here as long as Else has need of me. – I thank you though for your advice," she added apprehensively while they were already striding through the hall.

"It was meant well," the little physician said insistently.

His view of the girl's innocence no longer stood so steadfastly with him. He gauged his companion with a distrustful look.

They entered.

Wilms was sitting by the ill woman's bed, his head with its short cropped blond hair sunk low on his chest. He did not lift it either when he heard the girl's step. His large hand rested in that of his wife.

The consoling words of the doctor provided the relief to the stretched out woman, for she lay quietly now, and nodded eagerly to Hedwig to come closer.

The younger woman obeyed. At the same time, she felt that the ill woman's look was penetrating her, and although it seemed to her as if the silver ring which Wilms had gifted to her was now becoming white-hot on her finger, and even though she thought her lips would now confess by themselves the secret kiss, she forced herself nevertheless, and looked openly and calmly at the ill woman.

Only her breast heaved fearfully. The eyes of both sisters met, and when Else looked into those quiet, brown eyes, they seemed to create reassurance. At least, she drew Hedwig down to the edge of the bed, and stroked her cheek silently. But in bending down, Hedwig's garment skimmed the seated Wilms. A blow seared the young, excited woman. Again a moment had come when she had almost thrown herself across the suffering woman to throw the burden from her, and confess all her guilt. But the doctor's incursion forced itself between her thoughts. After the physician had conferred a few rules of conduct to the leaseholder, the faithful friend of the house said goodbye, and soon a quiet rolling announced that he was passing out of the yard.

The three depressed and burdened people remained alone. Deep, prolonged silence reigned, only occasionally did the sand on the floor crunch or the clock stir in its case and strike. The ill woman was lying down, and had closed her eyes, but under her lowered eyelashes, she steered her look furtively from Wilms to Hedwig, and from the girl again, peering at the man.

But her suspicion was fed no nourishment.

The two sat opposite each other as if they were completely unfamiliar and indifferent to each other.

"Would the old servant only have spoken from hate?" Else thought relieved, "Oh, if it were true though." A long time elapsed. Then Else noticed, playing in the manner of the ill nervously with the little gold heart on her breast, how her sister bent down over her as if she wished to talk with the man who was completely sunken within himself.

"No — no." The suffering woman did not want that. In the midst of her torment, she became jealous over the young beauty who sat so calmly on the edge of the bed with her white, rosebud-patterned dress flowing down her body light and close.

How fully she was blossoming. — No, no, she should not talk with Wilms. Else wanted to be alone with her husband. And now it also occurred to her how strangely Hedwig watched the gold heart. It infused the ill woman with fear.

"The heart — is — a keepsake from Wilms," she burst out with effort as she kissed the tiny treasure, "and now, Hedwig — go sleep. — Wilms shall stay with me today — I — I want to be alone with — my husband — do you hear?"

It was said so significantly, and accompanied by such unmistakeable antipathy that Hedwig rose quickly, and hurried out of the dull room of the ill woman without another word. She was hardly outside when she breathed out with relief, and fled up to the little room which she had been residing in again since Else's return.

Up there, she lit a candle, opened the window, leant out, and sucked in the warm numbing night air which poured in across from the meadows and fields.

"How long might she well live?" went through her mind again impatiently. She was now already waiting like a desperate woman. And as she knelt already half undressed on her bed, she stretched her arms out longingly once more as if she wanted to embrace someone, ensnare them insolubly to her breast. Ardour and desire washed all her fear away. Wild, without all containment, she lay in bed, and listened to see if Wilms would not come to report to her the elimination of the decaying woman.

A long forgotten song occurred to her. She hummed it to herself in her excitement:

> The black rider stops before the house.
> Come out to me fine lady,
> A shirt is enough – must hurry
> So that by the first light of morning
> I am back over sea and valley;
> We will ride many miles.

But the black rider did not stop before the farmstead, the hourglass was still running on.

***

It struck one.

The ill woman stirred. With moist hand, she still held the right hand of her husband. "Wilms," she whispered hoarsely.

Startled the leaseholder rose up. In his numbness, he had given way to slumber, and only noticed now that the expired eyes of his wife must have already been resting on him for a long time, dull and rigid.

"What do you want, Else?"

"I think – it will soon – be the end with me," his wife rattled, and it sounded as if death were already sitting on her breast.

"Else – for God's sake – have you become worse then?"

"Yes, I believe so. – Wilms – thank you for all your love – – – only lastly – but tell me the truth; you have never lied to me. – If I die now – will – will you then marry Hedwig?"

It seemed already as if her voice were penetrating from the other side of the grave, the leaseholder clasped the arms of his chair, he could not produce a single word, his tongue stuck in his throat, with barely any strength, he shook his head while the image of the more and more discoloured woman captivated his entire soul.

Slowly the parting woman raised her finger, and moved it in the way you threaten a little child. Then she motioned to him that he should bend over her, and while she kissed the ungainly man with dying passion, she whispered to him clearly, "Listen to me – Hedwig is nothing for you – you don't suit each other, – because – oh, because she is much more than you – and don't you remember, my poor man – don't you remember – what I told you – that time about Hedwig and the Count –". A satisfied smile played barely noticeable around the lips of the prone woman, this last revenge seemed to do her well, particularly when she sensed that her husband started as though smitten. Once more she opened her eyes to enjoy this picure fully, then she breathed out, "She is not pure – not like me – like me – – like – –"

The words faded away into emptiness, a new powerlessness took her away, and only for after a few moments did the tormented woman awake again, and cry out loud. Cold horror had seized Wilms, no, he was not capable anymore of remaining alone with the struggling woman. He sprang for the door, and called loudly through the house, “Hedwig – Hedwig.”

The girl was lying sleeplessly still up in her room, for she was expecting something similar, that Wilms would give her a sign.

Was it the end already?

A zest she had never felt before penetrated her, an eerily beautiful state, and yet her heart was throbbing like a bell, and fear poured over her with an unsettling chill. It seemed to her as if she were feeling the death pangs around her, as if the soul of the parted were flowing past her just then.

“Hedwig – Hedwig.”

It sounded so imploring. She shrouded herself scantily in clothes, and went noiselessly down the stairs. At the lowest landing, Wilms was standing, and staring upward.

“Is she dead now?” Hedwig asked, completely forgetting herself.

The farmer shook his head, but he probably did not comprehend her.

“Not yet,” he responded mutely – “but I cannot remain with her alone, – come in.” He opened the door, and let the girl step forward. Then they sat next to each other by the window, and looked wordlessly at the tortured body which could not live and could not die. The younger woman could not bear this mournful picture. Instinctively, and just following her strongest urge to intervene everywhere, she took the little bottle with the toxic sedative, and let the drops drip into the spoon. Wilms counted them with her mechanically. – “Five – six – seven.” The girl stopped, and poured the drink into the suffering woman, after which she soon fell victim to a leaden sleep.

But Wilms thoughts flew onward. “Would it have been a crime, if the ill woman had been offered the entire bottle?" he brooded. Then she would have finally found her salvation, she would have sunk into slumber so as never to wake again, and calm would have settled in the house, and peace.

A timid sideglance skimmed the girl sitting wearily next to him, and now the leaseholder noticed for the first time how firmly she was leaning on him so as to avoid the look of the resting woman. Strange – Hedwig's lips were moving quietly, it seemed as if she were counting the breaths of her sister. And in these minutes of silence, the leaseholder also saw that she was only clothed loosely and lightly, her beauty shimmered all over at him. He covered his eyes with his hand so as not to notice, but he saw it anyway. The woman who was rocking ever deeper there into sleep seemed in that moment as if she were already sunken and forgotten.

Quietly and softly, Hedwig nestled against him as if she wanted to go to sleep.

Both sisters were tired, very tired.

Wilms's mood became stranger and stranger. Then there was a quiet knocking on the door.

When the leaseholder opened it, he saw outside in the clear, starlit night, standing in full vestment, Pastor Schirmer whom Wilms had sent for at the dying woman's wish.

Silently he led the late guest into the living room. The clergyman must have plucked a twig from a blossoming pink hawthorn somewhere along the way. He placed it as a last gift on the white linen. Then the crucifix was set before the bed, the candles lit, and the trembling little man wanted to dispense the last rites to the drowsy woman. But the journey-ready woman lay silent and stiff, and heard nothing of what she would have usually absorbed passionately. But the prayers which the clergyman murmured to himself instead of the sacred rite were not spoken into the wind. If it was also lost on the one sister, the younger and more beautiful followed a clerical rite for the first time in a long time with restrained breath and burning eyes.

It seemed to her as if this were the wedding tune which would be held for her and the man next to her – close by the bed of the parting woman.

"Amen, – amen," the priest concluded.

"Amen," Hedwig repeated firmly and boldly.

The Pastor wanted to remain alone with Else, and so the other two went out quietly. Before the door, they remained for a moment, and listened. Inside they heard how the priest recited prayers with a loud, excited voice.

Then they parted without offering each other their hands, yes, without saying good night. So high had the tension between them climbed that they had nothing more to say.

It was still only an urge.

Tired and indifferent, Hedwig sought out her bed, and Wilms kept vigil in the dark, good room next to Else's room throughout the fearful, sad night.

Inside the trembling, old, little man sang ever more devotedly, and what the doctor's art had never been capable of happened there.

Else suddenly opened her tired eyes, and a rapt smile spread over her entire face. The deepest parts of her life were joined, and now rang out. Yes, she wanted to die like a child of God, like a pious woman. With untold effort, she straightened up, and clung to the clergyman with joy, "You – are – it, Pastor?" she breathed, "oh, how beautiful – – then it is well with me – oh, so well –"

And she laid her head devoutly against the old man's white head, and while she looked up through the window at the brightly flickering stars, she sang quite softly with her dying voice the song of resurrection with him:

Oh blessed who is saved then,
Who dies in the Lord, arbiter of men,
Oh blessed, who on leaving the road,
The city of God
That is up above have found.

Now open to us, gates of peace!
Here let the pilgrim's journey cease.
Ye quiet slumberers, make room
in your still home,
For the new stranger who has come!*

In the dark, adjoining room, a man sat, and heard everything which took place within. — Wistfulness, despair, passion climbed up in him, a spasmodic sobbing clustered in his throat; shaking, overwhelmed, he folded his hands, and stammered back what rang out to him.

He did not know anymore what he was praying.

XI

The last morning broke for the ill woman. Pastor Schirmer, the kindhearted, old clergyman, had promised the child of his parish to remain with her, and so the daylight streaming in found the blond woman in a deep sleep from which she awoke refreshed. To his astonishment, the Pastor learnt that the suffering woman felt better. Only that what she was saying seemed to him

* From "Wohlauf, wohlan, zum letzten Gang!" by Christian Freidrich Heinrich Sachse, second verse from the translation by Jane Borthwick (1855), "Hymn Sung at a Funeral" (first verse above was omitted from her translation, and is translated for the first time here).

to be excited, confused, incoherent, even her eyes blazed about restlessly over all the objects in the room. Her gaunt fingers moved in constant motion, and scratched back and forth at the bed cover.

"Hedwig – should come – and comb me – and wash me," the ill woman then requested, "and should – bring a mirror with her."

The clergyman shook his head with concern, but he sent for the girl anyway to say goodbye then himself with kindly words.

Wilms stepped quietly into the living room, but his wife did not notice him at all, and only when he timidly offered her, "Good morning, Else," did she smile gently, and look down at herself. She seemed to locate herself in her mind as being shortly after her wedding, for she whispered bashfully, "If I – have a child, – and it – is a girl, then – Hedwig shall – be godmother. – – Is Hedwig not here yet?"

And still in deep thought, she loosened her hair, brought it forward, and entwined a strand around her finger. When Hedwig finally appeared, both sisters looked at each other strangely for a long while. Else smiling gently and blissfully, the younger woman in contrast was frightened, and could not explain the picture to herself.

"Come, Hedwig," the ill woman whispered, seemingly freed from all pain, "wash and – comb – all this hair presses against my head – have you such soft hair too? – Look, I can envelop myself completely in it – Wilms always delights in it – – Hedwig" – here she hugged her younger sister tenderly, and caressed her cheek, "when you are a woman, you must always let it down too. – Then he will kiss it. –"

– And while she looked with her pallid face into the mirror, she hummed:

Ye quiet slumberers, make room
in your still home,
For the new stranger who has come!

But it was not a dance melody which she sang, and she made an impish face at her image in the mirror as if she found herself very beautiful.

Both the others looked at her, filled with cold horror. This was the most terrible thing they had undergone with the suffering woman up to now.

Hedwig fulfilled every wish of the ill woman with a gentle hand, until her sister suddenly started, and stared at the girl.

She had discovered something.

Then she looked down again at Hedwig's finger to finally let her blazing eyes glide over her caregiver anew.

She pondered for a moment.

"Hedwig," she began with singing voice, "what sort of ring is that you are wearing? — look, of silver — my husband always wanted to give it to me, and now he has given it to you — — look — are you his bride now?"

"Else — let go of my finger — it's hurting me."

"Are you his bride? — Come, Hedwig, I want to tell you something," she bent down, and screeched suddenly with a cutting voice, "Adulterer!" — Before the appalled man could free the girl from her clenched grip, the furious woman led Hedwig's hand to her mouth, and bit, as she also screamed loudly, into the ringfinger, and scratched and tore at her hair.

"Help — help," Wilms cried. With a spring, he was on the bed, lifted the girl high in the air, and hauled her half-numb body into the next room. She was trembling all over, and slung her arms around his neck, sobbing and begging for help.

Then Wilms forgot himself.

He gathered the girl, whom he was still carrying, to himself, and pressed full of sorrowful pity furious kisses onto her mouth, forehead and hands, as if he had to make good everything that was owed just then to the ill-treated woman.

"Hedwig, my dear Hedwig – great God – if only it were already over."

And his wish would be fulfilled. A strange rattling sound rang out behind them, Else, when she had been robbed of the younger woman, yielding to her sick, delirious brain, had sprung out of the bed, had in bare feet reached the door to the adjoining room and opened it.

There she saw the tableau, and heard the kisses.

Slowly she placed her arm on the cold wood, made a weak motion in the air with her other hand, and lowered her head as though tired onto her raised arm.

And she had also seen enough.

A rattle, a heavy, dull fall, her eyes closed, and a corpse was lying on the stone floor in a white shirt.

"Else – she is dead."

No answer.

Then the farmer threw the girl from himself, and stared distractedly down at the stiff shell of his wife.

The tenth hour of morning struck in the grandfather clock, a horse whinnied just then in the stable.

The black rider had fetched the fine woman in the white shirt, and chased thundering with her over the bridge which leads over into eternity.

***

It was after the funeral.

The mourners had gone away, and now the rentier Schröder, the father of both sisters, wanted to say goodbye. He looked very similar to the deceased, the old gentleman, despite his dignified, black frock coat, the militarily-parted, snow-white hair, and the tiny order rosette in his buttonhole. He walked sadly up to Wilms, who sat impassively in the corner of the sofa, and squeezed his hand melancholically, "God has placed a weight over us," he said uncertainly, "but we must submit to his will, my son – I would not have believed that I would yet experience it."

With that he drew out his white handkerchief, and cried bitterly into it. Gradually he got a hold of himself, and turned to Hedwig, who sat dressed in black by the window, and looked out dreamily across the yard over to the sunny country road.

"Come, Hedwig, my carriage is already outside, your things can be sent after you. I want now to at least have my only one around me."

She should go?

A paralysing wonder filled the girl; she had not thought of this possibility.

– And yet, it was so natural, she could not remain alone before the eyes of the world with the man in the bleak farmstead.

She rose. Demanding support, she looked over at Wilms.

But he did not stir. He did not sense how beautiful she was, he sat always with the same unmoving face, hunched in his corner, and looking silently and indifferently before himself. With the same air, he had in the past days let everything pass by him. The coffin, the corpse, the burning candles, the singing village children, the old dignified, stooped father, the clods of earth tumbling into the grave, nothing had been able to break this dull, sober silence.

But now – now, when someone wanted to wrest his beloved from him – then Hedwig expected something, and her eyes began to glow ever more yearningly – now he must throw all his memories from himself so as not to let the wife take his choice from him.

Oh, she was convinced he would now blaze up, now — — she listened and waited, only always the same silence.

She scraped impatiently with her foot.

"Wilms," she said softly.

But the man in the corner did not move at all, sombre pictures must have stood before his soul, for he turned his head, and stared at the place where Else had lain in her white shirt. Then she shivered.

"Come, Hedwig," her father urged. "It is time now, if we want to be back before evening."

The old gentleman picked up his hat, and looked once more, quiet and saddened, around the room where his daughter had died.

Then the girl took a deep breath, her entire figure straightened up, "Father," she responded quickly and definitely, "I cannot accompany you now, I must stay here still for perhaps a week because I promised Wilms to calculate everything in the business for him, and set in working order what was upset by Else's illness. But then," — and again she sighed strangely — "then I will follow you."

The rentier hesitated. "Another week?" he repeated confusedly, and wiped at his tophat. "So? — My son," he turned questioning to the farmer, "would you rather that Hedwig remained — remained a while yet? Yes?" He waited for a while, and since Wilms seemingly had not heard him at all, he must surely have considered this silence to be agreement, for he continued slowly and apprehensively, "Now, if you desire that — of course — you have also suffered such a great loss, that you long for company a bit, well, then Hedwig can stay here for eight more days, I have nothing against it — although, hm, yes, I desire only that you would become a bit calmer in time — and — now adieu, Wilms — and may we meet again in better circumstances, my son. Always chin up, you hear?"

Here the old official's voice wavered apprehensively, he turned away abruptly, and soon afterwards, he left there as the last mourner.

Hedwig and the leaseholder found themselves alone again.

In the first hours, Hedwig could hear her heart throbbing, it pounded so brightly and expectantly. "What would surely follow now?" she thought. – The path was free, the burden shaken off, dropped, finally there was nothing to separate them anymore, and she yearned with consuming violence for the strong man to now take her in his arms, and kiss and cradle her, still more tenderly and ardently than a few days before when Else had died over it.

But the day died away without the quiet man asking or desiring anything from her; he took his lunch silently, he cut short the evening, dull and dejected, to retire up to his room.

He had during that long period not exchanged a word with the girl. It was already pressing like an incubus on her breast.

The tall stooped figure was already at the door when Hedwig called him breathlessly.

"Wilms."

He stopped, but did not raise his look.

"Won't you – won't you walk in your fields tomorrow?"

The farmer nodded indifferently, and placed his hand on the doorhandle.

Now he would vanish.

It was crunch time.

"Wilms – don't you want to stay here?"

A timid look skimmed the beautiful creature, then it strayed past her, and fell on the large covered bed which once formed the home of the ill woman.

A powerful movement ran through the gigantic, ungainly body, he seemed to want to control and subjugate himself, but then Wilms threw both hands over his face, and a soft, stifled groan emanated across to the appalled woman.

It was the wild sobbing of a desperate man, a convulsing, comfortless self-accusation.

In the next moment, the leaseholder had vanished behind the door, and the woman left behind only heard how his steps echoed on the creaking stairs.

She stood there, and stared with fearful horror at the empty doorway.

Was it really true? – She found herself alone now? The man whom she wanted to lift, free, make happy, from whose sore shoulders she intended to take the burden of sorrow with soft hands under the pillows, he was fleeing from her? He made no word of appreciation?

She looked around the wide, brightly lit room.

No, no, in shadows, in returning spirits which floated about the place of sin, she did not believe. Wilms was just overwrought; under her care, his health would return, and the lust for life, and the lust for her.

Defiantly she drew the gold heart from her dress which she had taken from the dead woman with a firm hand, and read with her red trembling lips the name "Wilms".

Then she undressed, and without fear, with a strange, almost exuberant smile, she sought her bed, and decided to dream of Wilms.

No, no, the shadow was invoked, ghosts do not return again, the dead do not disturb the living, she confidently embedded her head on her white arm, and in the dream, which she directed at the beloved man, she smiled again her proud, seductive smile.

XII

On the next day, Christ's ascension was celebrated. For the first time, Wilms and Hedwig sat in the lilac arbour for coffee.

Humid, fuggy and warm air skimmed over the earth, trees and flowers stood motionless as if they were looking up fearfully at the grey clouds which were massing together there above the massive black mountains, the swallows circled around the barns in skewed, low flight, the dull silence before the storm left men and cattle silent, only the grasshoppers and frogs in the meadow droned and croaked louder than ever.

And something was also towering up silent and humid between the two people who sat soundlessly opposite each other in the arbour. Animated, and passionately tending to him, Hedwig had made everything ready and right for the leaseholder, he had also sometimes nodded his head as though in thanks, but now he was brooding again, his head propped in his hand, bleakly into the brewing storm which already hung from the heavens like an enormous black rope. Already solitary, heavy drops were slapping down on the lawn.

Then the farmer rose, and Hedwig heard him call for the coachman; at the same time, she also noticed that the wicker carriage was already waiting before the entrance.

"Do you want to go away?" she began apprehensively.

Wilms nodded.

"For business?"

Again the leaseholder lowered his head gravely.

"Will you be away for a long time, Wilms?"

Still the man's eyes timidly looked at the ground, but for the first time in days, he offered an answer. It came out clenched, "Yes, it may well – last a few days."

Then the girl rejoiced that she was the first to hear his voice again, and with overflowing emotion, she stretched out both hands to him to say goodbye to him.

But he did not touch her fingers. The tall man stood bleakly before her. His eyes under the bushy eyebrows remained rivetted, wide-eyed and rigid, on her rosy skin as if they could not part from the sight, but when he raised his head timidly, then he embraced the girl with such a mournful, discouraged, and spiritually shattered expression, his broad lips trembling so spasmodically, that the girl rocked back in sudden horror.

A cold fear ran through all her limbs.

Did she not see that the tormented man started several times as if he wanted nevertheless to grasp her hand, only to let his right hand soon fall again?

Just what was hindering him?

Something invisible, inexplicable must have regularly arisen before him, and with a sudden resolve, he tore himself abruptly away from the girl and, without another word, ran as though chased to his wagon.

The whip cracked, the horse pulled, and soon the woman who was left behind could hear how the carriage rolled away.

She leant weakly against the wall of the arbour, and looked slackly up into the grey, shifting heavens from which the thundershower still would not roar down onto the demanding land.

"So that is the end?" she thought. She grasped her forehead, and was startled. Her entire surroundings suddenly seemed so foreign to her; how could she have tarried so long in this bleak, accursed farmstead, she who had stepped out into the world with quite different hopes?

A long blinding flash went across the horizon; a dull distant grumble thrust itself inbetween, and a short downpour whistled over the land.

The trees shook themselves, and straightened up. Large drops pearled on leaves and stems.

But Hedwig was also refreshed anew, she had overcome her weakness. – She stretched her figure playfully, and strode with her powerful stride into the farm building to manage the servants calmly and confidently like before, and to take care of the small estate's business in Wilms's absence.

"Take the empty sacks there away from the window, Dörthe," she ordered with her fresh voice.

"Yes, Miss, they still lie there so that the blessed lady would not be disturbed by the rattle of the wagons."

"Well yes – but my sister does not need them anymore, we however could perhaps still have need of the sacks."

The people obeyed her. Absolute order and obedience without contradiction had come to the farmstead.

And Hedwig herself had won back her complete confidence.

She knew now that the dark spirit of melancholy was hovering over Wilms, that the dead woman had nonetheless arisen from the grave to drive the two who desired each other irreconcilably apart. But she did not take fright at the woman in the white shirt. The living woman had yielded before her, and hence she wanted to deploy all her strength to also chase the bloodless shadow from the house.

Outside the hard drops were striking against the farm building; from the grey walls of mist, it rolled and crashed dully down.

A hissing gust of wind whirled over the farmstead.

***

Wilms travelled along the country road. His goal was a pair of large estates in the area around Greifswald. When he came past the church of Boltenhagen, the sound of the organ and singing rang out so that he was jolted out of his self-absorption.

He was surprised by it.

"Jochen, what day is it today?" he asked his coachman.

"Yes, sir, don't you know? Today is the day of Christ's ascension."

Wilms clutched at his head.

Had he lost all conception of time so that he knew nothing at all about the high holiday? He had previously on this day always sat in the oak pews next to Else, and sung devoutly with her. – But since Hedwig had been at work at the farmstead – – – no, no, he did not want to think any further.

He quickly sprang down from the carriage, and strode hastily up the steps into God's house.

Perhaps his salvation resided here, perhaps here the miserable, cowardly fear could be taken from him.

The church was full to bursting. Just then the organ fell silent, and little Pastor Schirmer began preaching from the pulpit. Stirring and moving, he described the suffering and divine meekness of the Son of God, and how he, after his resurrection, appeared to the disciples, who did not recognise him in his white garment, by the Sea of Galilee to let them make the blessed catch.

"His countenance was like lightning, and his raiment white as snow."*

Then Wilms, who had taken a seat on the hindmost pew, was startled, blanching. The hallucination which had floated before him appeared again before his eyes; it went black before him, church and men turned in circles.

The stormy fear chased him from there.

He had to get out — in the air — in the open, so that he could breath. Swaying he rose.

Only the entrance of the leaseholder had been noticed by his neighbours. They whispered softly to each other how miserable, ill, and haggard the farmer looked, and the forester, Eltze, who was sitting near him, followed him out.

And just when he man struggling for air had reached his carriage, the kindhearted giant grasped the leaseholder's hand, and held him back.

"Wilms, are you ill?"

The leaseholder stared at the other man.

"Yes — Eltze — I can't — sleep at night anymore."

"Oh, nonsense, old friend, why ever not?"

"Because — because my wife is always with me."

"Wilms — for God's sake — old friend, you've merely talked yourself into it."

The leaseholder shrugged his shoulders, and as he climbed into his vehicle, he answered wistfully, "That could well be," then he farewelled the forester curtly, and in the next moment, the vehicle was rolling into the grey storm.

"Jochen, keep an eye on the gentleman," Eltze called after the departing men, full of concern.

And he was right about his warning, the kindhearted huntsman.

---

* Matthew 28:3.

The dark spirit which was shadowing the miserable man with its dark wings sank ever deeper onto its victim so that the night became even bleaker in him.

It twitched and flashed in the heavens, the narrow streaks of fire shot in long lines there, the thunder rolled out of the dark cloud bases, and echoed over the broad plain.

Thus the travellers arrived at an inconsiderable lake which intercepted the main road with an arm of water so that it had been bridged at this place.

From the bulrushes and reeds which surrounded the unmoving water, damp, grey fumes were swelling up; the surface lay pale and colourless; alone by the bridge, a pair of stunted silver willows rose up.

Just as the vehicle rattled over the rotten wood, Wilms was passing his glance indifferently over the silent lake.

But then – the leaseholder straightened up, and stared across at the shore on the other side.

He must have seen something terrible, for cold feverish sweat broke out from all his pores; with his hand, he grasped the shoulder of his servant.

"Jochen," he cried, "turn around."

"Lord – Lord Jesus – what is it?"

"Jochen – Jochen – turn around."

The coachman began trembling all over, "Sir, you are surely ill? What is there across the lake? – Tell me – I am frightened."

But the farmer emitted not another word. With wide eyes, he stared across the grey surface, for the bleak spirit which was over him was painting an appalling picture.

Over there stood a female figure, her shirt was "white as snow", her eyes flashed like glaring lightning, and above her a crashing thunderclap discharged loudly.

Then the servant started to become terrified of the staring man; with all his strength, he turned the horses around, and chased back along the path he had come amidst pelting rain with his powerless passenger.

***

Two long, fearful weeks elapsed, then the leaseholder could leave the large bed in the living room by which Hedwig had stood watch day and night.

It cut everybody's heart when the formerly so gigantic man straightened up weakly, and looked himself in the mirror with a wistfully smiling look.

"Well, Wilms, now fresh air," fat Dr Rumpf cried – "and then, child, the window open, and something decent for the stomach – – a few bottles of red wine, and the main thing: out, out!"

And Wilms let himself be led on the physician's arm into the garden in which the lime trees were now blossoming, and spreading a refreshing, spicy scent.

"Oh, it is beautiful here," the farmer said as he sat in the arbour admiringly, "come, Hedwig – and you too, doctor, we will remain together a while."

The other two threw each other a meaningful look, and intended to cheer him up a little with harmless conversation, but the leaseholder did not let them get a word in.

He was more talkative than he had been for years. Everything surrounding him in nature reminded him of events from his youth, from his apprenticeship, and also awoke memories of his mother.

"Do you still wear the ring, Hedwig? – You will always revere it, won't you? Do you still remember – that Christmas Eve?"

Only Else was not mentioned. It seemed as if the grave now held her firmly, as if the earth had finally closed over her permanently.

When the physician rose after some time, Hedwig followed him, and asked quickly and desperately, "Well, doctor, well?"

"Yes, what shall I say? – Nourishment, my child, nourishment. That is the sole means above all."

"Yes, but doctor, he eats almost nothing at all."

"Hedwig," the physician spoke gravely, and caressed the girl's hot forehead, "now everything depends on you, do you understand?"

"No."

"The man is spiritually ill," the doctor said slowly as he looked her firmly in the eye, "do you understand now why everything depends on you?"

Then the girl turned pale and then dark red again, and looked at the floor in front of the old friend.

She understood him.

"And tomorrow, I will come again," the physician called in a different tone, kissed his young friend's hand in farewell, and left the farm.

With glowing cheeks, Hedwig ran into the garden, now she knew what the experienced doctor demanded, that she should leave the man she loved. – She – she herself was held to be the reason that he could not achieve any peace; was it possible that her presence tormented and tortured him? – Did he really think himself burdened with sin because he had preferred her blossoming life to the dying woman? – The dead woman won, the dead woman roamed the house, the dead woman maintained her place at his side. – No, she could not let herself be driven away like that. – She sat down fawningly next to Wilms, and when he smiled encouragingly at her, she slung her soft arms around the emaciated man, and whispered with her fearful shaking voice, "Wilms, I love you so much, is it true that you are well again now?"

And as her lips were placed on his, it seemed to him as if a precious, refreshing, healing drink streamed into him, filling all his limbs with a pleasant indolence so that he leant his head wearily on her breast, and strove to fall asleep there.

"Yes, Hedwig," he murmured refreshed, "now we will soon be very happy."

"And is it true that you don't think of Else anymore like before?"

"No, no, Hedwig – leave it – I don't think of my wife anymore – don't want to anymore – only you."

Was it the blossom of the lime trees which the gentle wind rocked from the branches, was it Hedwig's closeness, the weary man slumbered placid and secure on her respiring chest like a calmed child.

A black mockingbird was nesting above in the crown of the lime tree. It sang the lullaby.

But the thought of the separation demanded of her consumed and bored further into the girl.

***

Another time, the ill man looked attentively and thoughtfully at Hedwig's proud, white neck, from which a slender, golden chain was hung.

"Hedwig, you aren't wearing there – – – ?"

"Yes, Else's gold heart."

"You own that?"

"Yes, I took it from her."

The leaseholder rested his head, and looked musingly before himself.

"I like it," he said finally, "that she did not take it with her into the earth. – Then it would have always seemed to me as if my heart had been buried. – But now it lies thus with you."

Then he stretched his arms out, and pulled her to himself. And they both embraced each other as if they were seeking safety from the white shadows which passed inexorably through the house.

And when she nestled ever more passionately in his arms, it passed like a tremor through the ill body. "Hedwig — Hedwig," he stammered, "I will — surely never again be completely happy."

Then the girl glowing with love felt a chill, and understood him.

***

The state of Wilms's soul became more and more doleful. Often, if Hedwig came in the door unexpectedly, she met him then as he was staring at the doorway in which Else had once sunk down lifelessly, and when she then flew to him to encourage him with her love, then an expression of fear came into his eyes as if her tenderness were tormenting him.

And one time, he forced out the words with difficulty, "Hedwig, don't kiss me like that — it always seems to me as if Else is watching."

Then the girl started, and whenever she approached him in the following days, she always thought she felt something cold and chilly skimming past her.

She clutched her forehead, and began to smile achingly. She was beginning to believe in ghosts.

In time, the ill man also began to mix Else's name more and more frequently into his conversation. Sometimes he recalled the words of his wife, other times all sorts of peculiarities, and one day, at lunchtime, Hedwig noticed that the leaseholder was observing her with wide, horrified eyes, "What is it, Wilms?"

"You — you look — very similar to her," the farmer stammered aghast, and let his knife and fork clatter from his hand.

And in the afternoon, Hedwig perceived from the adjoining room that Wilms, instead of sleeping, was sobbing bitterly to himself.

Against that she was incapable of anything. The dead woman had prevailed.

Her wonderful, splendid body blossomed next to him, and the ill man cuddled and jested with the decayed one.

***

"Uncle doctor," Hedwig wailed when she sat in the arbour with the white bearded physician she had had fetched, "what shall I do about it?"

She had confessed to the old friend everything which she had lived through in the past year at the farmstead.

"What should you do?" the old gentleman asked, and placed both the young, feverish creature's hands in his own. "Hedwig, my child, I am fond of you, and fond of Wilms, and hence I say you must go away."

She stared at him with her large, brown eyes, and the physician felt in her hands how the blood hammered and shot in the veins.

"Still, child, still," he said, "you don't want to ruin him, and look, as often as he sees you, he will always see in you the cause which drove the deceased to her death. – No, no, my child, stay calm, I know you love him a lot, but just because of that, Hedwig, I ask you, free the poor fellow from all the nasty memories. Believe me, as long as you stay here, the dead woman will also stay with him. – You've noticed that yourself, haven't you?"

Hedwig lowered her head, but she nodded gently. Then she looked with a wistful glance out at the blossoming garden, at the adjoining, lush meadow, at the distant fields in which dust rolled past, shone through by the sun.

She had worked and achieved things everywhere here. She had won back order and abundance. The dead woman had not been capable of that.

Amidst her tears, a defiant smile drew over her pale face.

"Now, Hedwig," the physician asked, and stood up, "Do you know now what you have to do?"

She was still soaking up the picture of the blooming fields; with shaking breast, she was sucking the fresh country air into herself. Yes, she had prepared everything for a prosperous future, but she would not enter the promised land.

"Hedwig?" the doctor asked more urgently.

"Look, doctor," the girl cried as she pointed with her hand at the beautiful estate, "I ordered this seed, see over there the green stalks? But someone else may harvest them," she whispered with choking voice.

Then the old gentleman stroked the young creature's wavy brown hair from her hot forehead, took her in his arms, and as her sobs obtruded on him, he said, as though to a small child, "Right – right – you are a brave, little thing, everything will turn out well again."

***

"Hedwig," Wilms said on one of the following days as they sat together after coffee in the living room, "you are dressed so elegantly, are you wanting to go for a drive?"

The girl looked at him earnestly for a long time as if she wanted to impress on herself every one of his features, then she shook her head, smiling bleakly, but she turned away, and let her eyes rest for a long time on the yard, and looked over in farewell to the poplars by the country road.

After a while, she turned her beautiful face to the stooped man, and asked simply and yet full of dammed-up sorrow, "Wilms, have you really grown a little fond of me?"

"How can you even ask that, Hedwig."

"And more – more than Else?"

"I beg you, child – you must not mix in that – let her rest."

He knitted his brow, and shook his head weakly.

"Are you angry at me?" Hedwig suddenly cried passionately, and when she threw herself on her knees before the chair of the stooped man, she embraced the ill man, and lifted herself up to him, "You aren't angry with me, are you?" she whispered with a wavering voice, and nestled up to him, "I did everything merely out of love for you, you know that, Wilms?"

The farmer was stirred. "Yes, my child, yes," he said lovingly, and caressed her golden sparkling, brown hair.

Then Hedwig slowly stood up, and looked once more attentively around the room. Then she stepped quickly to the piano to play something for Wilms, as she was already accustomed to doing about this time. Tired and weak as he was, the notes still rocked him easiest of all into the yearned for slumber.

"What shall I play?"

"All the same, they are all beautiful."

"No, what do you like."

"Well, then the one from Christmas, you know, Hedwig."

She closed her eyes, a sweet shiver passed through her for the last time. And then she played the old folk-song which had already sung away an infinite amount of weariness.

Outside a carriage was rolling down the main road, Hedwig's heart pounded to bursting, but she did not let any of that be noticed, and bravely played the old song, so gentle and wistful and mourning, so that tears entered the eyes of the ill man, who did not know yet what stood before him.

And he fell asleep really gently and smiling as the song of farewell quietly concluded. When he awoke, the room was empty. Everything was still, only from the country road could you hear the dull beat of hooves, and the rolling of a vehicle hurrying away.

***

The forester had taken Hedwig in his wagon to the train, and looked up at her admiringly in the carriage.

Fiery and blood-red, the sun rose in the sky; it poured over the girl rosily as she peered out the window at the district in which Wilms's house lay.

But the farmstead had long ago sunk behind the fir copse, and strangely, as Hedwig now leant out the window, she was again the distinguished, young lady who had arrived at this place more than a year ago.

She did not comprehend herself; since the dreary, leaseholder's house had disappeared behind her, fresher air had streamed towards her, it seemed to her as if she had herself lain infirm for a year, and would now for the first time go out into the laughing, sun sparkling world again.

"Where are you going now, Miss Hedwig?" the forester asked.

"I don't know. – Anywhere where there is something for me to do and to make. – The world is large."

"You are right there. – And will you perhaps come back here soon?"

"That could happen too. We never know what the next hour will bring."

The bell tolled. – The forester waved his green hat.

"Give my regards to Wilms," Hedwig cried, breaking out into tears.

The train moved, and it travelled quicker and quicker into the golden-red fervour of evening.

Hedwig did not look back anymore.

About the Publisher

Our mission is to provide translations into English of the complete works of neglected major European writers. We do not cherry-pick works that seem the most marketable, but rather seek to provide a complete collection of each writer's works so that readers can follow the writer's development and decide on its merits for themselves.

http://www.facebook.com/KANitzPublishing

www.ingramcontent.com/pod-product-compliance
Lightning Source LLC
LaVergne TN
LVHW101940220826
846093LV00006B/74

* 9 7 8 0 4 7 3 2 8 2 3 5 6 *